The beginning? The end? Or somewhere in between?

No one had made me kill Senna. I did it because I'd wanted to. Because I believed it had to be done. I still believed that. And yet with every passing moment, with every step I took, the guilt became nearly overwhelming.

Oh, please god, I just wanted out of Everworld. There was no place for me here. Go back home and forget it all happened. That was my impossible dream. Because in the real world it would never be okay that I killed Senna. In Everworld, it had been necessary. . . .

Look for other EVERWORLD titles
by K.A. Applegate:

EVER WORLD

ENTERTAIN THE END

K. A. APPLEGATE

SCHOLASTIC INC.
New York Toronto London Auckland Sydney
Mexico City New Delhi Hong Kong

No part of this publication may be reproduced in whole or in part, or stored in a retrieval system, or transmitted in any form or by any means, electronic, mechanical, photocopying, recording, or otherwise, without written permission of the publisher. For information regarding permission, write to Scholastic Inc., Attention: Permissions Department, 555 Broadway, New York, NY 10012.

ISBN 0-590-87996-0

12 11 10 9 8 7 6 5 4 3 2 1   1 2 3 4 5 6/0

Printed in the U.S.A.

First Scholastic printing, May 2001

FOR MICHAEL AND JAKE

ENTERTAIN
THE END

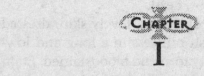

CHAPTER I

Seven of us. Seven survivors. All that were left of the horror.

Standing on a hilltop overlooking what was left of Merlinshire. Merlin the Magnificent had led us there, out of the castle through a tunnel that led from the keep and under the moat. Merlin. A powerful wizard but chastened now, and worried. Like all of us, unable to ignore the grim reality of what we had just witnessed.

The almost total annihilation of Loki's forces — Loki, the Norse god of destruction. The swift and sure murder of his son, the giant wolf, Fenrir. And the almost total destruction of King Camulos's forces. His murder. The triumph of weapons' technology over bows and arrows, over the brute force of the trolls and the impossible size of a mythological creature, which, in Everworld, was real.

Standing slightly behind Merlin were Etain, the half-elfin Irish princess, and her elfin mother, the queen, Goewynne. Homeless, driven from their kingdom, from Merlinshire. Father and husband, King Camulos, dead.

Etain. Red hair, blue eyes, lovely skin, dressed like a fairy-tale Irish princess in a long and low-cut dress, now badly torn and bloodstained. Etain was genuine Irish-maiden charming but so much more. She was smart and curious and savvy and politically aware, definitely the daughter of the king.. Now the daughter of a dead king. An exile.

And Goewynne, who was until that morning the benign and powerful coruler of Merlinshire. Goewynne might remind you of a society lady but without the pretentiousness, just the sophistication and graciousness, the deep awareness of her place. She was physically beautiful, with long, shiny black hair and pale blue eyes that now looked gray with sadness. Goewynne had been devoted to her husband.

Now Goewynne was a widow, face swollen and bruised from a Sennite's blow. Still, somehow, she managed to retain an air of royalty. I couldn't imagine the effort it must have taken for her to stand so tall when the ordered, peaceful society of Merlinshire had been destroyed, crushed by the technology of a more advanced and civilized society. That was a sad and sick irony.

Merlinshire had been a lovely port town of Ireland, at least the Everworld version of Ireland. Picturesque wharf, a park, houses built of limestone with thatch or slate roofs. Cobblestone streets, busy little shops, even a cable car system. Now it was all gone. All gutted and burned, its citizens tortured, murdered, driven from their homes.

Ireland. It was the nicest place we'd visited in Everworld so far. Home of the Tuatha De Danaan, sacred isle of the Daghdha. Except now the Daghdha was dead, killed by Ka Anor.

Still, even without the Father God, Everworld Ireland had thrived for two hundred and nine years in peace. Ever since the Peace Council had met at the Magh Tuireadh. Ever since the residents had chosen to follow Merlin's Way.

Ireland had thrived for more than two hundred years until we showed up. Four kids from the old world. Followed by Senna and her insane tribe, bringing weapons unlike any Everworld had ever seen and turning them against Ireland's people.

Four kids from a suburb north of Chicago, Illinois. Dressed in a bizarre and filthy assortment of clothing that had long since ceased to resemble anything from the Gap or Tommy Hilfiger.

There was David, our leader because he needed to be, because we needed him to be. The responsible one. The hero. The one still in possession of Sir Galahad's sword. Beaten and bloody and bruised but standing.

Jalil, our scientist, the voice of reason. The smartest. Brave, too. Ruthless, unsentimental, and self-serving when he had to be — but utterly trustworthy. He'd saved my life on more than one occasion, at no small risk to himself. Now, his spirit was broken by the public humiliation Senna had cruelly sentenced him to suffer. He stood stoically, staring directly in front of him.

And there was Christopher. He'd carried Etain from the castle, through the dark, dank stone tunnel and released her only when we'd reached the hilltop. Only moments before Christopher had been under Senna's spell, ready to betray us all, his gun aimed at my head. But he was free of Senna now. He was wounded and discouraged, but one of us again.

Finally, there was me. April O'Brien. Led from the castle by Goewynne, taken by the hand like a person in a trance, a person stunned and in shock. Led to the hillside, away from the scene of the crime.

April O'Brien. Pretty decent citizen, good in one world. Murderer in another.

There were only four of us now because Senna was dead.

I had killed her.

CHAPTER
II

We stood, the seven of us, transfixed, up on a hilltop, up by the windmills, looking down on the charred ruin of Merlinshire. We were responsible for introducing electricity to Everworld. We were also responsible for introducing the notion of gunpowder to this place of bows and arrows and magic.

But Senna alone was responsible for this ultimate devastation.

We looked down at the damaged walls of the once magnificent castle, a structure right out of a medieval tale.

At the remains of Fenrir's carcass. The impossibly large wolf with the power to draw the four of us and Senna into Everworld. With no great effort he had been shot dead by a gang of real-world sociopaths.

We watched the fleeing trolls, Loki's soldiers, most of whom had panicked and run as soon as they saw Fenrir fall.

We noted the bodies we could see and those we could only imagine. Among them, Senna's. And the burned body of the Sennite follower she'd killed as an example of her might.

And where was Loki? Had he run, abandoned his troops, saved his own butt? Loki was a coward. All along he'd wanted to run away from Ka Anor, back into the real world. Close the gateway after him.

Actually, maybe Loki wasn't a coward after all. Maybe he was just really smart.

He wanted out of Everworld.

And so did I. . . .

Everworld.

After all the time I've been here and I still don't know how to describe or explain it. It was a universe unto itself but parallel with the real world. A place of myth and story, where thousand-year-old legends walked and talked and sometimes died. Where gods of every culture known in the real world — ancient Greek and Roman, African, Aztec, European — cavorted and fought and fiddled with human lives. Where humans lived alongside elves who traded with dwarfs who avoided trolls who were strange but not half as strange as satyrs.

Everworld was a physical landscape that made no sense in relation to our real-world understanding of geography and ecosystems. A landscape stitched together like a patchwork quilt, deserts jutting against brown northern European fields on one side and lush Mediterranean seascapes on the other.

Everworld was a universe that supported all sorts of life-forms, humans and gods and all varieties of real-world creatures, as well as those from other planets. Ka Anor and his Hetwan followers. The Coo-Hatch. Probably many others.

It was a world where time passed on a whim. Sometimes too fast. Sometimes too slow. This was a place where up was usually down and down was up — or sideways. Where dragons far too large to fly flapped their tiny wings and floated away.

And now the reason for our being here in Everworld, in this open-air lunatic asylum, was no more. The person responsible for our being dragged across the barrier between universes was dead.

And we were still here.

CHAPTER III

We were a sad and silent troupe. None of us had spoken since we'd left the castle. What was left to say?

We walked and I was alone with my thoughts. I had committed a murder. It had taken place in the context of battle, but that didn't make the fact any easier to bear. It didn't make me any less guilty. Or afraid.

Senna was dead and nothing was the same. *But now it's the way you wanted it to be, April, right?* my brain taunted. *This is what you've always wanted. Senna gone, Senna out of the house, out of your life.*

It was true. I had wanted Senna dead. I had hated her beyond reason. Oh, I had a long list of *actual* reasons for hating Senna, but none of those could really justify wanting her dead.

Or could they?

An eye for an eye. A life for a life. I should be dead, too. Someone should take my life in exchange for Senna's.

But there was no one to avenge Senna's death. No one had cared for her enough to seek justice for her murder. Keith and the other Sennites? They were too damaged for true devotion. Senna, their leader, was gone. Fine. She was weird, man, anyway, a seriously scary chick. They'd go on raping and pillaging and playing target practice with anything that moved. No loss.

Even David, poor David, he had loved Senna, but even David knew that in some way it was better she was gone. He would never admit that to himself, but he knew. He wouldn't retaliate against me for what I had done. If he did anything it would probably be to himself. He'd berate himself for not having saved her, protected her, rescued her from her own dark fate. Everything was always David's fault. In his own mind, anyway.

Christopher and Jalil? Merlin? Etain and Goewynne? They weren't sorry Senna was dead. Maybe they even admired me for killing her. They weren't cold-blooded, any of them; they also must have felt some pity for me, some sympathy. Senna's half sister had been forced to kill her.

It's weird. When Senna and I were growing up, there had been no frame of reference to help me understand her. To feel any sympathy or love. She was so different from me. So different from most people. In ways I can name and in too many I can't. Yes, we lived in the same house for years. Yes, we shared a biological father. Yes, we were almost the same age.

But all that didn't really mean anything. Senna and I weren't really sisters. And we weren't friends.

Senna was a stranger who wound up living in my home, sitting across from me at the dinner table, next to me in church, a stranger who shared the backseat of the car when we went on vacations. Why? I don't know. I wanted to ask my mother. But I couldn't. I knew she hated Senna as much as I did. And she was as helpless as I was to resist the power of Senna's discomfiting presence.

I could ask my father, I decided once. I could ask him because his guilt had made him vulnerable.

No longer the incorruptible, hero father, now he was just a man.

"Why is Senna here, Daddy?"

"Because it's the right thing to do, April. I thought your mother and I explained that to you. It's our — my — responsibility."

Well, how could I argue with that? And then — just like now — I went around in circles. Trying to figure it all out. Trying to figure how my feelings got me to this point.

No one had made me kill Senna. I did it because I'd wanted to. Because I believed it had to be done. I still believed that. And yet with every passing moment, with every step I took, the guilt became nearly overwhelming.

Oh, please god, I just wanted out of Everworld. There was no place for me here. Go back home and forget it all happened. That was my impossible dream. Because in the real world it would never be okay that I killed Senna. In Everworld, it had been necessary.

CHAPTER
IV

We came to a stream. But before I could use my hands as a cup they had to be cleaned. Silently I stuck my bloodstained fingers into the icy water. Watched, fascinated, as the blood softened and slicked away.

Beside me, Jalil knelt. Held his own stained fingers under the water's surface until they were free of blood. Then he bent over and splashed his face with the cold water. He held his hands there, over his eyes and nose and mouth, for what seemed like a long time.

"We should rest for a few minutes," Merlin said. His voice startled me. No one had spoken for so long. No one questioned him now.

After I'd drunk my fill, I walked back from the stream and sat down, head on my knees, arms wrapped around myself. I tried to rest, but my brain was wired too tight, every nerve stretched too thin for peace.

I lifted my head and saw David standing, facing back toward Merlinshire. His face betrayed his disbelief. It also betrayed the fact that he knew some of the answers.

I wanted to reach out to him, offer comfort, and yes, take what comfort he could give me. But David was too far gone, too far away to be touched right now. Least of all by me.

"We should have brought the body with us," David said. "We should have buried her someplace. We shouldn't have left her there with those idiots. . . ."

I felt someone put an arm around my shoulders. I turned my head. It was Christopher, crouched at my side. Ordinarily, I'd be wary of such a gesture on his part. Christopher was not above trying to cop a feel, even in a moment of sadness. Well, the old Christopher, anyway. He'd changed. We all had. But somehow the changes in Christopher seemed more obvious than those the rest of us had undergone.

He proved this now by giving my shoulders a gentle squeeze and singing, softly, ironically, "So no one told you life was going to be this way . . ."

He made me laugh. But, it came out to be more of a sob.

I looked over at Jalil, sitting close to the stream. The blood was gone but his face was still darkened by long, deep scratches. His own doing. Because Senna had made him attack himself.

Jalil. He'd known what I was going to do, almost at the same moment I discovered my own intention. He'd thrust Excalibur into my hand, his Swiss Army knife outfitted with Coo-Hatch steel. Superb metal, able to easily cut any substance. Jalil had ripped through a wall with that knife, that tiny blade. Ripping into flesh was far easier. For the knife, anyway.

I put my head back down on my knees and sighed. What had I felt in that moment, that moment when the blade penetrated Senna's flesh? I didn't remember, maybe couldn't. Maybe it was better not to remember but a part of me wanted to know. Was I exalted with a sense of divine duty? Was I crazy with rage, was it a crime of passion? Was I clearheaded and sure or panicked and doubtful?

And, I remembered wondering, for a split second, calmly, curiously, if Senna's blood would kill me the way it had killed the patches of grass in Africa. Remembered Thorolf affirming that, yes, a witch's blood was poisonous. We had threatened to use Senna's blood to destroy the sacred tree that united the two halves of the African Everworld.

But nothing had happened to me. The blood had covered my hand, a witch's blood, my half sister's blood. I had watched it slick and dark against my pale skin. And I'd lived.

Suddenly, sitting there on the banks of that little stream, I remembered a million little facts about Senna. A million little details I'd never bothered to list and review. Why should I when she was always there? Now that she wasn't I couldn't seem to stop the torrent of facts that comprised the person named Senna Wales. How she drank coffee black. How when she sneezed she always sneezed at least three times in a row. How when she was twelve she wore her hair in a loose ponytail straight down her back and made it look sophisticated. How for a while she wore a small silver star on a black cord around her neck. How one day, it was gone.

Hundreds of insignificant details, details that belonged to Senna alone. It was like learning all you could about a character you were going to play on stage. Almost as if gathering every seemingly arbitrary detail could finally put a person together.

But it didn't work. I couldn't construct a person out of my memories of Senna. At least not a person I could understand. Her personality, her character, her motives and dreams and emotions — nothing.

In life, Senna was an enigma. In death, she remained an enigma. At least to me. And I guessed to everyone. Especially David.

CHAPTER V

We rested by the stream for a while, then set off again. Sheep and stone fences and rocky fields. A harsh Celtic landscape, not far from the cold gray sea. When we came across a dolmen, an ancient place of burial that was marked by three large rocks — one resting horizontally across two standing vertically — Merlin and Goewynne created an illusion they promised would camouflage our temporary campsite from the roving bands of Sennites.

We were hungry, cold, and tired. Three conditions far too common in Everworld. I couldn't remember when I'd last eaten or slept. I'd have probably given my right arm for a bowl of hot soup.

It was pretty obvious that we were all ready to talk. About some things, anyway. David called a meeting. I couldn't imagine a meeting undertaken with less enthusiasm and such a strong sense of despair and defeat.

No one mentioned what I had done to Senna. No one.

"This is what we do now," David said, his voice harsh, words slightly garbled by a swollen lip. "We made a promise to Athena. Nothing's changed. We go back to figuring out a way to defend Olympus against Ka Anor's Hetwan."

"Maybe we should take a nap first," Christopher muttered. "A very long one."

"Maybe not just a nap, but some time out."

They were the first words Jalil had spoken since we'd fled Merlinshire. The first time he'd lifted his head, met any one of us in the eye. Now he spoke to David.

We'd always wondered what lay at the core of Jalil's relationship to Senna. What hold she had had on him, before he'd somehow broken away, infuriated her with his independence.

Now we knew. Senna had shown us in the most cruel and crude way. She'd publically humiliated Jalil, shown his enemies and his friends that he was a victim of his own mind, a prisoner of his own head. She'd laughed and pointed while Jalil had obsessively, compulsively pantomimed washing his hands. While he rubbed them raw, clawed them and then at his face.

Jalil was proud and unsentimental. I'd always known that about him and respected it. I would never mention what we'd seen. Would never say I was sorry. My sympathy wasn't what he needed. What would bring Jalil back to us was something concrete for him to do.

"Come on, guys. We don't have the time to waste," David said.

"I'm not talking about wasting time," Jalil answered. "I'm talking about us finding a place to hide out, somehow begin manufacturing our own weapons. It's not impossible. We look for even one Coo-Hatch, one of them who hasn't gone back to his or her own world yet. They owe us, man. We make a deal with them, we start our own weapons tech center. From there we build the greatest army Everworld's ever seen. Won't be easy but get what gods we can on our side and take down Ka Anor."

I watched Jalil as he spoke. I admired his renewed determination. But it made me feel suddenly so very, very tired. Was I the only one who just wanted to leave this, this *place* for good?

David nodded. "One of us scouts for Coo-Hatch. The rest . . ."

"No," Merlin interrupted. "Don't you see? If you build an army, one big enough to be noticed and feared, you will just become the new threat to the gods. They will never join you to fight Ka Anor. Instead they will turn what lazy, unorganized energies they have toward fighting you. They know — or believe — that fighting Ka Anor is a losing battle. They will trade the terror they know for the terror they *don't* know. They will strut and bluster and believe they have found the opportunity to assert their might."

"That doesn't make a whole lot of sense, now does it?" I said, surprised I cared enough to comment. "But I think Merlin's probably right. The gods are inherently fixed, narrow personalities. They're not going to suddenly change, see the light, join us, whatever."

"Here's what I'm thinking," Christopher offered. "I'm thinking the Sennites are a way bigger threat right now than the Looney Tunes we've been calling gods. These guys are without a real leader anymore, which probably means lots of infighting, major civil war. Remember, these guys are not all that bright and most, if not all, are certifiable. I'm guessing they're stuck here in Everworld, now that Senna's gone. Got to be some panic in the ranks. I'm thinking, a group of Hetwan approach these guys, they're gonna leap at the chance to sign up under a big macho guy like Ka Anor. This dude eats gods? Cool. Let's join up!"

"Christopher's right about that," Jalil said. "The Sennites are stupid enough to sign up with Ka Anor. But before they get themselves toasted by alien forces, they're going to help the Hetwan cause some major damage."

"We're looking at the worst possible scenario," said David. "Only way to prevent it from coming down is to divide and conquer. Take out one group, then deal with the other."

Christopher rolled his eyes. "You think? And it sounds so simple when you lay it out that way."

"It's not a plan," David said defensively. "Just what we have to do."

"Have to *try* to do," I murmured, surprising myself again. Because I didn't want any part of this place anymore. I really didn't.

CHAPTER
VI

"Look, we're refugees," David said. "It's a lousy fact. We're a pitifully weak band of seven survivors. We need help. And if the gods are too unreliable to be our true allies — and they are — then we have to turn to mortals."

Christopher snorted. "We can forget about Everworld humans. Just about every one of them we've met is a poor, downtrodden peasant. Those folk are used to being raped and pillaged, not to fighting back."

"'As flies to wanton boys are we/men to the gods.' Shakespeare," I said.

"Right." Jalil nodded. "And to rally people who've been abused since the day they were born would take way too much time, something we have way too little of. Besides, there's still the question of how to arm them against Keith and the Sennites. Against rifles and pistols and Uzis."

"Hey! We're right back to where we started, how about that?" Christopher asked.

"I feel certain I can rally my fellow elves," Goewynne said halfheartedly, "but there are far too few in Everworld to turn the tide of this war. We will need others."

"Okay, how about the fairies?" David suggested.

"I can't believe you've forgotten, my friend. Or are you just that desperate? Fairies work only for cash. They don't do favors, they're not into volunteer work, they don't give to charity." Christopher paused for just a second. "You know, that's what I like about fairies. The Everworld kind, anyway. They are opportunists. They are all about looking out for number one."

"However obnoxious his presentation might have been, he's definitely got a point," Jalil noted. "Fairies work for money. We have no money. No collateral. Absolutely nothing of value to trade. Not a damned dime."

"Dwarfs." David again. He wasn't going to give it up.

"What about the dwarfs?"

"They're all that's left. They're our only hope."

"How do you figure?" Jalil asked.

"Dwarfs have money. Particularly, they have gold. We need gold. With enough gold we could hire all the fairy archers we want."

"Yeah." Jalil's eyes narrowed. "And finance a weapons factory. Dwarfs could probably even make the guns for us. I mean, if we come up with something we have that they want."

"Ah, there's a problem," Christopher said.

"And here's another one," I said. "The dwarfs really don't like us. The Nile, remember? We sort of set fire to their dam? Lots of crispy bodies floating around?"

Merlin frowned. "A few truths about dwarfs it would be well to remember. They tend to stay out of the affairs of other peoples. And they never forgive an injury or insult to one of their number. They never forget it, either. I doubt they will work with you. They would probably prefer to dispose of you."

"Okay, let's say they surprise us," David said.

Christopher sighed. "Didn't you just hear what the man said?"

"Could happen they work *with* us. So we're back to what do we have that the dwarfs want," David said.

"Dwarfs want gold," I said wearily. "Strike one."

"The dwarfs want me." Etain.

"What?" Christopher said.

I saw Merlin nod to Etain, then close his eyes. A gesture of acceptance. Maybe resignation.

"The dwarfs want me," Etain repeated. "At least their king, Baldwin, wants me. For his bride."

Christopher barked a laugh. "Which one, Billy? Alec? How many brothers are there, anyway? I'll tell you this. At least one too many. And he is *not* marrying Etain."

Goewynne looked at Christopher, pity on her face.

Etain spoke softly. "Dwarfs prize elfin women, Christopher. Almost as much as they prize gold."

"Okay, all right. I can understand Mr. Baldwin's point," Christopher ranted. "I mean, if the dwarf women look anything like the dwarf guys, I mean, okay. Got it. However, and I do mean this in a pleasant way, no freakin' DWARF is marrying Etain. Okay? Over my dead body."

"This is Everworld, Christopher," Jalil said. "That could very well happen."

Christopher made an exaggerated frown. "Oh, yeah, I forgot. Everything's been so peaceful and all for so long, I just got lulled into la-la land over here. Look, man, I am sick to freakin' death of these gods. These freakin' idiot gods. Why can't they get their act together, huh? Can anyone answer me that? No, I didn't think so. We're surrounded by all these gods of war, Huitzilopoctli and Neptune and even David's favorite, Mistress Athena, and none of them, NONE of them do any real fighting! Oh, excuse me, some do. Sometimes. Only they do it badly. On the wrong side!"

"Are you finished?"

"No, I'm not finished, General Davideus. In fact, I'm not sure I even got started."

"Save it!" David snapped. "It's not helping."

Before Christopher could respond, Merlin spoke, his voice stronger than it had been.

"Thor would fight," he said. "As would Baldur, Odin's favorite, most beloved of the gods of Asgard. And the mighty Odin One-Eye, too." His voice fell. So much for hope. "But the All-Father is imprisoned by Loki. And great Thor and courageous Baldur, both are lost, their whereabouts unknown."

"Merlin, my man," Christopher said. "Prepare for your world to be rocked."

"We've seen Baldur and Thor," David explained. "Hel's got them. Baldur *and* Thor, they're each frozen in a huge block of ice."

"And not one of us is too excited about the idea of descending to Hel's psycho harem," Jalil said. "Even for almighty Thor."

Merlin looked amazed.

"But don't you see?" he said. "If Thor were freed and reunited with Mjolnir, he would help us free Odin. Together the two most powerful Norse gods would assemble all Vikings to the battlefield. The Vikings, along with the elves good Queen Goewynne can rally, would be the start of a magnificent army!"

"We don't doubt that," Jalil said. "But Merlin, the fact still remains that the Sennites have guns. We'd have to arm Odin's forces with something that would enable them to fight back. I mean, successfully. Without being just plain slaughtered."

"Yeah," Christopher added. "How about a fair fight for once?"

"It could be a fair fight." David gripped the hilt of his sword. He looked more animated than he had since we'd ran, tails between our legs, from Merlinshire. "Dwarfs."

"Again with the dwarfs? Are you fixated on short, stocky men in chain-mail shirts, David? 'Cause I would have pictured you with the tall and lanky type. . . ."

David ignored Christopher. "Like Jalil said, the dwarfs could forge weapons. Assuming we can get them to work with us, make a deal."

I glanced quickly at Etain. She seemed lost in thought.

"And they could cut a tunnel into Hel's domain," David said. "Ka Anor's Hetwan failed but . . ."

"Large and Crusty," Christopher said, "Nidhoggr, man, he's a bud. He's on our side. He might not actually help but he probably wouldn't stand in our way. I mean, if we run into him down there. And what am I doing talking about going back to Hel? It's lack of food. Sleep. I'm delirious."

Jalil folded his arms. "What exactly is your plan once we're in that psychopath's harem, David? I seem to recall our not doing so good last time. Horror, panic, nauseating scenery. In fact, I seem to recall that unfortunate experience about every other hour of my life."

"The attack distracts her," David said, like it was a done deal. "Hel would never expect an invasion, especially by us. So, while she's freaking, some of us slip past and rescue Baldur and Thor. Then get the hell out of there. No pun intended."

A beat of time passed, as everyone absorbed what it was we were crazy enough to be planning.

Then I shook my head. "No, David. Merlin, listen. It's insane. We can't go back there. You saw. You remember. Hel must be furious we escaped once. Do you really think she'll let us get away a second time?"

"I don't think it would be a good idea to give her a choice," David answered, eyes narrowed.

"Oh, don't be such an idiot!" I shouted. "You're a guy. A, that means you're probably dumb enough to go back up against the worst thing we've faced here, thinking, *Hey, this time I'll show her.* And B, it means you're powerless in Hel's presence. No one's doubting you're brave, David. But you're not indestructible."

"Sometimes I think he is," Jalil muttered. He and David exchanged a look. Smiled.

"Well, golly gee whiskers," Christopher said brightly. "What do we have to lose but what's left of our sanity?"

Merlin didn't back me up. It was decided.

"There's still the little matter of what to exchange for the dwarfs' help in getting into Hel and then manufacturing weapons for the cause."

I could tell David felt awkward saying it. But he had to. I wasn't going to bring it up again. Neither was Christopher. Jalil might have.

Etain spoke. "I will marry Baldwin."

"My daughter." Goewynne laid her hand on Etain's arm. She'd lost her kingdom, her home. Worse, she'd lost her beloved husband. And now she was losing her daughter. And still she retained an air of grace and dignity and calm. "Are you certain?"

"Yes. It is what I must do."

It didn't look like marrying Baldwin, the dwarf king, was what she wanted to do. Etain's beautiful face was paler than usual, her blue eyes dark.

"No way!" Christopher cried. "I thought this was settled. Etain, you can't do this!"

She smiled fondly at him. "Just because you don't want it to happen does not mean it won't," she said. Then she took his hands in hers. "Christopher, you must come to see that this self-sacrifice is necessary."

"But you don't love the guy! Have you ever even met him? I mean, he's a dwarf! Do you even have anything in common? What are you going to talk about at dinner every night! I mean, maybe this guy is a slob. Maybe he's a real pain in the ass. Maybe . . ."

"Yes, maybe. But he is an old dwarf, by dwarf standards. He will live only another ten years, perhaps twenty, if he is lucky."

"Twenty years! But . . ."

"Do not worry, Christopher. I am part elf. That heritage will protect me from physical change. I will not have grown older."

"Yeah, that's great, Etain. Really. But that's kind of not the point. I mean, you'll be all peaches and cream but *I'll* have gotten older. I'll be, what, thirty-seven? Oh, my god, I'll have a potbelly. I'll have gray hair. I'll have ear hair! Jeez, twenty freakin' years! What am I supposed to do with myself for twenty years? Sit around and wait for your husband to croak? Wait for him to achieve the eternal horizontal? Twiddle my thumbs until he decides to take a dirt nap? This is so not going to happen."

I didn't have the heart to tell him that yes, most likely it was absolutely going to happen.

Chapter
VII

We formed a plan. Goewynne would set off to rally her fellow elves. She would go alone, relying on her native swiftness and magical abilities to keep her safe until she reached Fairy Land. It seemed the best place for her to start. From there she would go where necessary and in one week's time, meet us at DaggerMouth, King Baldwin's castle. According to Merlin, the castle was the only external, visible part of the dwarfs' ancestral Everworld home. The Great Diggings was otherwise entirely subterranean.

Merlin would leave us, too. His self-appointed task was to search for Thor's mighty hammer, Mjolnir. The last time any of us had seen Mjolnir was back in the land of the Aztecs. It might still be there — somewhere. It might be in the temporary possession of another Viking warrior. Either way, Merlin would retrieve it so that Thor's power would be restored. When we broke him out of Hel's domain, that is.

Merlin would also prepare a dramatic diversion to take place in Hel's underground lair. Something that would force her to heel. He didn't tell us more than that, no details of what he had in mind. Only said he'd meet us and Goewynne in a week, at Baldwin's castle. Merlin was tired, but he was still magnificent. And I trusted that whatever he sprung on Hel would be serious. But would it be serious enough?

The rest of us, including Etain, would journey north to DaggerMouth and, once there, present our offer.

Goewynne and Merlin would leave in the morning. I got the feeling they stayed for us, particularly for Etain and for me. Honestly, I was glad for the company of two wise and powerful adults.

We settled on the stony ground, wrapped in our stained and ripped clothing. We smelled of smoke and blood and fear and sweat. Etain was on my right, Goewynne on my left. Merlin, Jalil, and Christopher formed a tight ring around us, basically outside the protection of the stone "roof." David took first watch, as was his habit.

I lay there in the thick dark, eyes wide. Afraid

to sleep. Afraid to find I could no longer wake in the real world, afraid that now Senna was dead I'd lost all contact with the real-world April. Except for memories that would slowly drive me crazy with loss.

Around me, the others slept or pretended to sleep. Nobody tossed or grumbled or snored. Either we were all too tired to move or just too scared of being discovered. Or both.

VIII

I slept. Woke in the real world to lunch at the Rave Cafe. Magda and I. I saw we'd been shopping. Again. Bebe. Guess. *How much stuff do I need?* I asked myself. I wasn't even curious to see what I'd bought.

Only then did I remember I was glad to be here, Everworld April united with real-world April, in a suburb north of Chicago. Only then did I remember that I'd fallen asleep worried I'd been listed persona non grata in my real life.

Magda was talking about something she'd read in the latest issue of *InStyle*. At least, I think she was. My body sat across from her at the little marble table, but my mind was in Everworld. I got the breaking-news update and had to wrap my feet around the legs of the table to prevent myself from jumping up and screaming.

The final battle at King Camulos's castle. The spectacular defeat of Fenrir. Deaths, blood, fire. And Senna.

I'd killed Senna. I had killed my half sister. I had stuck a knife into her heart.

"That guy, David Levin?"

"What?!" My voice came out too loud. David's name was the first thing I'd really heard Magda say.

Magda gave me a look. "Don't shout, I'm right here. David Levin. Kind of cute but way too serious. Drives that old wreck."

"Yeah? What about him?" I said. Keeping my voice low and normal. I took a sip of the cold mint tea in front of me.

"It's like he's fallen off the face of the earth or whatever. I can't get in touch with him. He hasn't been in class."

This was not good news.

"How long has he been gone? I mean, you know, how long's he been out? Sick or whatever."

Magda shrugged. "A few days. I don't know. Most of the week, I guess. I mean, I wouldn't care, he's not exactly my type or anything, except that he's supposed to be my project partner and he's screwing me over royally by not showing up in class."

"Did you call his house?"

Magda rolled her eyes. "Yes, April, that had occurred to me. But once I got the machine and the
second time, two nights ago, I got his mother."

"And?"

"And she wasn't too happy I'd called. She
didn't really tell me what was wrong with him.
Come to think of it, she didn't really tell me anything. Just said that when she saw him she'd tell
him I called. And then she hung up. Probably
thought I was some hoochie mama after her pre-
cious little darling. Mothers."

CHAPTER

IX

I got away from Magda as quickly as I could. Made up some bogus excuse about having to run an errand.

"How come you didn't tell me earlier?"

I shrugged. "I forgot. Sorry, I'll call you later, okay? Here's some money to cover the drinks. I've got to go."

"Your bags!" Magda called out after me as I hurried to the door.

"Keep them for me, will you?"

I shot around the corner. Hoped that when Magda came out of the cafe she wouldn't see that my car was still parked across the street. Hoped she wouldn't find out I was a murderer. I was pretty sure that would be a good excuse for her to end our friendship.

I'd forgotten my cell phone. Try finding a

working public pay phone anymore. Not easy. I
found one, finally, and made the call. Mrs. Levin
was home.

When I hung up, my hands were shaking. Had
to find Jalil.

Mailboxes, Inc. Where Jalil worked now that
the Boston Market place had closed. Weighing
packages had to be better work than slicing
chicken. Cleaner, at least.

It took me ten minutes to get there. I pushed
open the door. A middle-aged man with a serious
paunch was at the counter. A pretty brown-haired
girl was explaining mailing options to him.

I spotted Jalil by a shelf of assorted-size Jiffy
bags. Walked over to him, didn't say hello.

"David is missing."

He flinched a little.

"I didn't see you come in. And what do you
mean, David is missing?"

"Missing, like he's not been in school."

Jalil shrugged. "I know that. I just thought
maybe he's sick. Or playing hooky, though that's
not the Mr. Levin I know."

"Jalil, he hasn't been home, either."

Jalil looked over at the counter. The brown-
haired girl was still talking to the middle-aged
customer. No one else had come into the store.

Jalil turned and motioned for me to follow him into the back room.

"Are you sure?" he hissed.

"Pretty sure. My friend Magda called him the other night about some project. His mother rushed her off the phone. Then I called on the way over here. She was polite to me but worried. And angry, too, I think. Said she hadn't seen David in days."

"Different schedules? Maybe he's avoiding her."

"No. She said no food was gone. No clothes. I think she wondered the same thing. She's been checking for any sign of him. Jalil, he's gone."

Jalil nodded. Like he accepted David's disappearance was something big.

"Are you here?" he said. He looked straight at me. "Did you get the update?"

I felt hot tears burning against my eyelids. "Yeah," I whispered.

"Are you all right? I mean . . ."

I shook my head and wiped at the tears that had started to flow. "No. But I will be. I hope. I don't know."

"April. Look, don't panic. I have to show you something. It's been freaking me out but I figure, hey, there's an explanation, I just gotta find it. I mean, this is the real world. Things work a certain way, always have, always will. Right? But . . ."

"But what, Jalil?"

He shook his head. "I don't know, man. I'm thinking . . . with Senna dead and David missing . . . I really don't want to be dealing with this but I'm thinking Everworld is seeping through. Or maybe Everworld Jalil is . . . just look."

He pulled me behind a large stack of folded cardboard boxes.

Began to unbutton his blue Oxford shirt, fingers trembling. Eyes on the door behind me.

"No, I'm not pulling a Christopher," he said when he saw the look of doubt that flitted across my face.

"Sorry." I wiped away the last of my tears.

He pulled the shirt open. Lifted his white T-shirt.

And there it was. A hole, right through the middle of Jalil's chest. Not a gunshot wound. Not some bloody, ragged, blackened hole burned there by Hetwan venom. Not the awful mark of a sword. Just — a hole. Clean, round, an emptiness all the way through his skinny chest. Like Jalil, real-world Jalil, the guy standing right in front of me, was a drawing and someone had erased a six-inch hole in his chest. Like he was a tall puzzle with one perfect piece punched right out.

Through the hole I saw a six-inch-round segment of a Priority Mail box.

Impossible. In Everworld, maybe. But impossible here, in the real world. Right?

Obviously not.

I stepped back from Jalil. Couldn't help it. After all the grotesque creatures I'd seen, after all the disgusting wounds I'd treated, this — nothingness — was somehow the most disturbing.

I. Was. Afraid.

"Have you told the others?"

"No. Haven't seen David, obviously. Didn't think of talking to Christopher about it. You're the first. Feel special?"

I laughed nervously. "What's going on, Jalil?"

"I don't know. Are you okay? I mean, whole?"

"I think. I guess. I . . . I didn't notice anything when I got dressed this morning."

"Any ideas? This might be more your terrain than mine," he said wryly. "I am pretty sure modern medical science is not going to account for a peephole in my rib cage."

"When did you first notice the . . . I mean, did it just appear that way or did it start really small . . ."

"Yesterday. At least, when I went to take a shower yesterday morning, it was there. Wasn't there when I went to bed the night before.

Though I was exhausted, got undressed in the dark. . . . Point is, it's new. And it's here whether Everworld Jalil is or not. That's something new. It's a kind of crossover we haven't experienced before."

"Senna," I said flatly. "It has to be. Everything always comes back to Senna. David's gone. Now this. When Senna died something must have happened to us."

"But you're fine, right?"

"So far," I admitted. "If you can say being simultaneously consumed with guilt for killing your half sister and also glad you killed her, wishing maybe you'd done it sooner, if you can call that 'fine.'" I sighed. "Look, I'll find Christopher, see what's going on with him."

"Yeah. While I go back to work comparing UPS to Federal Express to Priority Mail prices. I'm not out of here until six. Then I'll go by David's, see if he's shown up. Damn, I thought we were done with that witch. But I think you're right, April. I think maybe Senna's death is gonna cause consequences, the action and now the reaction. It makes no sense but neither does a hole in my chest. Senna dies in Everworld, we're the same in Everworld, we're experiencing weird stuff here, in the real world. At least I am. David could still be just A.W.O.L."

"No, I'm sure he's not hiding out on purpose."

I felt a surge of raw hate flood my body. Senna was dead and still she dominated our lives.

"You know, April," Jalil said. "What happened back there, in Merlinshire. At the end, when she was torturing us."

Jalil paused. I wanted to step forward again, maybe touch his arm. But I didn't. I wasn't sure he'd want me so close when he told me. Plus, I was still trembling with anger.

"My mind. It's not right. In the real world, I mean."

"Jalil, you're brilliant. You're intellectual and smart in so many ways and you're brave. . . ."

He laughed. Not a happy laugh, but not completely cynical, either.

"Thanks, I think. Obsessive-compulsive disorder. No one at home knows. Senna caught me once, before this all started. She caught me at school, in the lab. April, for one split second, she made it all stop. She made my mind quiet. I was in control."

"How?" A stupid question.

Jalil shrugged. "How did she do any of the strange things she did? Point is, for that one split second I was free of the disease. It was . . . it was beautiful. And I could have stayed free. All I needed to do was become her slave. Pledge myself to Senna as her unquestioning champion."

"You said no."

"Yeah. And she hated me from that moment on. It only got worse, of course, every time I fought her will. But I hated her, too. At the end, April, if you hadn't killed her, it would have been me."

I smiled and this time, I did touch his arm. "Except for the fact that no man could kill Senna."

Jalil grinned. "There was that. Anyway, in Everworld, no OC. From the very beginning, it was just gone. My world was turned upside down — sometimes literally — every fact I'd ever known and every theory I'd ever proved since the day I was born was being shown as false in this new place. I was frustrated and angry and determined not to bend to this new reality of chaos and uncertainty. This shifting version of reality, whatever, I still don't know what to call it. But still, I was free. In the one way I could never be free here."

I knew, at that moment what he was about to say.

"Are you saying you want to stay in Everworld?" I asked. "I mean, if it comes down to a choice. If . . ."

"If I fade right away here, would I miss it?" He gestured mockingly at the shelves of packing materials, rolls of tape, stacks of colored construction paper. "All this?"

"Yeah."

"I don't know, April. I really don't. There are my parents. And sisters. And Miyuki, she and I, you know, we're getting close. But there's the OC. And everything here, it's not the same anymore. Now there's Everworld, always in my mind. Memories that won't go away. I see everything here now so differently. Things I had tolerance for once, no more. This ordered universe, the rules I know by heart? It all seems somehow dull. Not enough. I just don't know. It might be too late for me, this world. You know?"

Chapter X

I ran. Literally ran across the street, cars honking at me, kids on a school bus sneering. Borders. Borders had bathrooms. I had to know. Now.

Grabbed the handle of the revolving door, pushed, too fast, the person in the compartment ahead of me looked back like, "What's your damage?"

I mouthed "sorry," tried not to make a mad dash for the bathrooms. Wouldn't look too cool, would probably elicit a few witty comments from the so-important college guy at the information counter. "Too much coffee in the cafe?"

I got on the escalator. Gripped the rail just like my mother had always told me to do. Didn't walk up the moving stairs, stood still, both feet on one serrated step. The real world being so full of dangers, unlike Everworld. Real-world April being so much more timid than Everworld April. Ever-world April would probably have climbed the rail on hands and knees.

Finally, second floor, stepped off, carefully. Walked deliberate-casual to the far right corner. Pushed open the door.

Every stall door open. Look at that, I had my choice. Chose the stall farthest from the door. In case I screamed or something, slightly less chance of my being heard. Went inside, closed and locked the three-quarter door behind me.

Okay. Examining my body is not something I do a lot of. But this was necessary. I hung my bag on the hook on the side wall. Took off my coat. Lifted my arms and pulled my ribbed cotton Gap T-shirt over my head.

Closed my eyes. Took a deep breath, and told myself, *It's okay, April, it's okay. Just look.*

I did. Nothing. I mean, everything, everything was there, where it should be. No magic peepholes.

Strained my neck trying to see over my shoulder. Looked like skin all around. Felt my butt. All there. Maybe a bit more than last month but oh, I'd never worry about an extra pound again, flesh was good, it was very good.

I got dressed, trembling slightly, relief washing over me. Then I sat on the toilet and put my head in my hands and cried.

CHAPTER
XI

"April, hey. What are you doing here?"

"Hello to you, too."

"Sorry. Just that you've never dropped in before, you know, unannounced. Without being part of some bizarre scheme to catch a Nazi-wanna-be arms dealer."

"Could you maybe shut up?"

"No one's home but us chickens. Come on in."

I followed Christopher into the den. The TV was on, of course. I noticed now that the remote was still in Christopher's hand. Of course. On a small side table, a can of soda and an open bag of Cheet-os. Of course.

Christopher flopped into the recliner and gestured toward the couch. "So, to what do I owe this pleasure?"

I sat on the couch. Instinctively pulled a pillow onto my lap.

"Are you here?" I said.

"Real-world me is here all alone. I'm awake over there now. But if you're asking if I got the update, oh, yes. The whole stinking mess. Right up to this crazy-assed scheme to invade Hel. About Senna . . ."

"I . . ."

"I'm sorry she got to me again, at the end," he said in a rush. "I was going to give you up, April. I know it wasn't really me but still, I'm sorry. I felt the moment she died. I was released, just like that. I'm glad she's dead, April. We all are. She had to die, you know that."

I nodded, unable to speak. Let a few tears well over and trickle down my cheeks. Then I took a deep breath.

"David's missing," I said.

"What do you mean?"

"I mean, he's gone, missing. I don't think his mother knows where he is. He hasn't been at school, either. Jalil's going by his house later to check again."

Christopher shrugged. Back to the old who-gives-a-Flying-Walenda jerk. "Hey, maybe he and Senna have hooked up on another astral plane.

Corulers of their very own bizarro kingdom. I bet right now David's showing her what he can do with his sword."

He punched the remote. An old Clint Eastwood movie. Clint was a cowboy.

"You don't seem very worried," I said.

Christopher shrugged. "I'm not. I have my own problems."

New station. Cartoon Channel. *Johnny Bravo.*

"*Love* this show," Christopher murmured. He was staring at the screen, eyes squinted, face intent. Like he was trying to burn the images into his head.

"What problems?"

Christopher sighed. Like I was bothering him.

He lowered the volume on the TV. Put down the remote.

Glanced toward the door of the den. Then he sat forward in the recliner, perched on the edge, and lifted his T-shirt.

"Like this. If you must know."

I should have known.

"Well?" he said. "Interesting, isn't it?"

I nodded, silent. Felt sick.

"When were you planning on telling us about this?" I said finally.

Christopher was fading. His chest was translucent, not completely, but not completely opaque, either.

"Only started a day or two ago. It's kind of an Invisible Man thing," he said, dropping his shirt. "Pretty soon I'll be wearing a trench coat, slouch hat, and dark glasses to school. I might even consider a life of crime. Bank robbery, unarmed of course. A cat burglar, maybe. Very dashing."

He sat back in the recliner but didn't pick up the remote.

"Jalil," I said. "It's happening to him, too. I mean, there's a hole, a perfectly round hole right through his chest. I mean, you can see right through it."

Christopher grinned. "Playing doctor with Mr. Spock, are you? So, how about you, April? All there? Maybe you should, you know, let me examine you, just to be sure."

"You're an idiot," I said. But I wasn't really mad. Christopher was just on autopilot, telling the old jokes, playing the old roles. I knew him well enough by now to know he was freaking, trying to hang on to sanity, like the rest of us. "I'm all here," I said. "I'm not fading, there are no holes. And before you say it: Only the ones that have always been there."

"Am I getting *that* predictable?" He laughed. "Time for some new material."

"What are we going to do?"

Christopher shrugged. "Nothing. For now. What can we do? You know what's interesting, though?"

"What?"

"I'm kind of able to control it. Now, don't laugh, but TV? The more I watch, the more into a show I get, like a block of reruns of *The Andy Griffith Show,* whatever, Barney Fife and Opie and Aunt Bea, the more solid I get. Doesn't last. An hour later, I'll be doing something else, I check, I'm see-through again."

I thought about that for a second.

"When is it going to stop?" I said. Rhetorical question. How could any of us know? "Someone's going to notice."

"Just one of several questions, April. Like, why is it happening? What's causing it? Why isn't it happening to you? And how am I going to explain a see-through chest to a date? I'm in even bigger trouble if another, er, vital part of me disappears. If you know what I mean."

Chapter XII

I woke groggily, a stone jutting into my kidneys, cold dew thick on my face. The sky was gray.

Around me the others stirred to life. I sat up.

"Merlin's gone." David. "So's Goewynne. We talked before they left."

"They didn't happen to conjure up a big pot of hot coffee, did they?" Christopher said, climbing stiffly to his feet. "And a bottle of aspirin. I ache."

"You also reek. We all do. Again." Jalil.

Beside me Etain raised herself to a kneeling position. She looked beautiful even now, tired, dirty, and hurt.

"Look, there isn't much point in hanging around," David said. "No food, the Sennites too close. We'd better get moving. Merlin told me the way to DaggerMouth. It's about a day's walk. Maybe a day and a half."

"Provided we don't get ambushed or lost or otherwise killed," Christopher grumbled. But he reached for Etain's hand and helped her to her feet.

We started to head north. I hurried to walk ahead with David. I was almost afraid of him, knew he might not want to deal with me alone, but I had to know.

"David. Did you sleep?" I said.

He didn't look as if he'd slept. His face was puffy, eye still swollen almost shut, split lip beginning to scab over.

"Yeah."

"Did you cross over?"

He shot me a strange look. "Why?"

"Because you're gone, David," I said urgently. "You've been missing, back in the real world. No one's seen you for the past few days. What's going on?"

He considered. "Yeah, that would explain it."

"Explain what, what?"

"I slept, but it wasn't like it usually is. I dreamed. You know, like we do — did — over there. But then, I also had these weird sensations, kind of like I was a ghost or something. Like I could go places and see things but nobody could see me. I was home, April. I saw my mom, I talked to her. But she couldn't see or hear me." He shrugged.

"You don't seem very concerned," I said. "David, you could be really gone, forever."

He looked at me like I was insane.

"I'm not gone, April. I'm right here."

His answer infuriated me. "Do you know about Jalil and Christopher?" I demanded. "They're fading over there. Parts of them are gone, David, just gone or fading away."

"What about you?" he said.

"I'm fine. So far. I mean, it could happen to me, too. David, I don't want to disappear! That's my life over there, that's the real world."

"Maybe for you that's the real world," he said. "I don't know, Everworld is real enough for me, April. Look, I don't know what's going on, but there's nothing I can do about it. I've got a job, to get us to DaggerMouth, negotiate with Baldwin, build an army. Get back to Olympus. Destroy Ka Anor and the Sennites. I really don't care that I'm not sitting in history class anymore."

"What about your mother? She must be freaking out!"

David smiled darkly. "Yeah, she's probably worried, a bit. She'll get over it. I was kind of a rock in her shoe. With me gone, she can get mar-

ried to her boyfriend, live her own life. No more
having to take care of her moody son."

"That's mean."

"That's the truth. At least the way I see it."

I stopped walking and let David go on ahead
of me.

Suddenly I felt as desolate as the landscape.

What had I done to us?

"Jalil!" I joined him as he passed. "I told David
about you and Christopher, about what's happening to you in the real world. He knows he's
missing, I told him that, too. He said last night he
dreamed. And was also in the real world but invisible, like a ghost. He doesn't care, Jalil, I do."

Jalil looked down at me with something like
pity.

"I still don't know what we can do about any
of it, April."

"I'll go to see Brigid." I said. "Maybe she'll
know what's going on. Maybe she's got an idea."

"Good luck. But I don't think it will help. Remember the last time you talked to her, she pretty
much said she couldn't stop Senna and her band
of loonies. Her powers are limited."

"But maybe now that Senna's gone . . ."

I fell silent. Jalil was right. At least right now
there was nothing I could do to bring David back
to the real world, to stop Jalil and Christopher

from fading away. But I made a vow that the next time I woke in the real world I'd try to see Brigid.

We walked. It was an uneventful journey as Everworld journeys go. Which was a welcome relief but also disconcerting. Everything seemed too quiet, too calm. Like everyone had gone into hiding, too afraid to be caught unguarded by this new menace — the Sennites.

How sick was it that I almost hoped for a minor skirmish with a randy satyr or lumpish ogre?

The weather was the only real difficulty. That and hunger, but we were so used to inadequate supplies of food by now it seemed like the normal state of things. The air was gray and damp and chill. A fine drizzle, more a mist, really, kept the rocky ground somewhat slick and made our clothes feel heavy and uncomfortable. And at the same time, inadequate protection against the elements.

After approximately fourteen hours of walking we reached DaggerMouth. No mistaking our destination.

"Check this out!" Christopher said, then whistled.

Rising from the relatively flat and stone-paved terrain like an ugly but impressively sized growth — DaggerMouth. Behind it but also somehow part of it, a series of five large hills or small mountains, each distinct in overall shape and size, but each rugged and rock-strewn.

DaggerMouth. An appropriate name for the thing looming ahead of us.

It was an intimidating structure, both a castle and a gateway through to the Great Diggings. A place, Merlin had told us, where King Baldwin and his court lived and where caravans of dwarf traders set out and returned home, day after day.

"Let's keep moving," David instructed. We did. And the closer we got the more certain I was that DaggerMouth was made entirely of steel. The walls, the towers, the guard stations, even, I later learned, the floors, everything was steel. The place looked like its name, a frightening and dangerous maw.

Images from movies raced through my mind. Jaws from the James Bond movies, that big hulk with a mouthful of wire. Hannibal Lecter wearing that terrifying face mask in *Silence of the Lambs*. God, even the Abominable Snowman from *Rudolph the Red-Nosed Reindeer*. A funny image now, but to a five-year-old those teeth were very scary.

"Cool," Christopher said. "*Very* cool place."

"Yeah," Jalil said. "Like something a brilliant kid would make with a seriously sophisticated erector set. And a macabre sensibility, definitely."

"I think it's truly ugly," I blurted.

Christopher grinned. "That's because you're a girl. Girls like white castles and pretty horses with flowing manes and pink puffy dresses. Right, April? Chain mail, steel, gray all over, not your thing."

"I agree with April," Etain said. Then, softly, she added, "Though I suppose in time I will come to appreciate the charms of my new home."

That wiped the grin off Christopher's face.

Chapter

XIII

We had reached the guarded main entrance of the castle, a jagged arch of, what else, steel. The keystone was decorated with a design in relief. Later I found out it was a fancy representation of a pick and ax, King Baldwin's family coat of arms.

I could see into the main courtyard. It was teeming with dwarfs, all male it seemed, everyone focused on a task, loading and unloading carts, checking papers, taking inventory of stacks of produce and bolts of plain dark fabrics. There was also a steady stream of dwarfs disappearing through several low-ceilinged tunnels at the far end of the courtyard. Slipping into the Great Diggings like two-legged moles.

I didn't get to see much of the Great Diggings itself until later, but when I did, I was amazed. It was a complete underground city, with crowded urban areas and less congested suburban parts, industrial sections and recreational parks. There were forts and barracks and storehouses for weapons. There were huge private homes and densely packed apartment buildings. Reservoirs, mine shafts — complete mining and refining operations — construction sites, and factories. Breweries and food processing plants, mushroom farms, and bakeries. Except for the herds of bats being raised for food, everything you would find in an average aboveground city but underground, lit by coal and oil lamps that vented through incredibly high ventilation shafts that allowed in only the tiniest pinpoints of sunlight. The whole thing was really a vast underground maze.

The Great Diggings was a bustling, cosmopolitan place. What it lacked in charm it made up for in industry. Jalil later explained to me that the complex extended throughout the Five Hills. Each hill supplied a particular metal and only that metal. One hill was rich with gold. Another, with silver. The third with iron, the fourth with nickel. The fifth hill supplied copper. Impossible, of course, in the real world, it made no geological sense, but W. T. E. Welcome to Everworld.

Two dwarf guards approached us. Each had his hand on the hilt of a broad, daggerlike weapon. Each looked very businesslike.

"Identify yourselves and state your business," the first one demanded.

"Pleasant fellows, the dwarfs," Christopher whispered, gently pushing Etain behind him but keeping hold of her hand.

Dwarfs. We'd run into them all over Everworld, it seemed. Even in Egypt, where they probably shouldn't have been — one, because they were a European myth, and two, because they were damming the Nile and subsequently causing the population to starve.

They weren't human but they weren't Hetwan, either. Their heads were oversized. Their legs were short and thick, their feet large. Arms short and hands huge and rough as if from hard work. They had massive shoulders and barrel chests. Their faces were elongated. Some wore heavy beards.

Generally speaking, the dwarfs — at least the men, we still hadn't seen any women — wore a sort of supple body armor, chain-mail shirts that hung to their knees, brown leather pants, and wide leather belts worn over a shoulder like a sash.

"I am General Davideus," David said, stepping forward from our little mob. "I am in the employ of the goddess Athena. I have been sent by Merlin to speak with King Baldwin about a matter of great urgency." He paused. The guards seemed unimpressed. Clearly, the habit of name-dropping meant nothing to them. So then David said, "And I am responsible for the burning of the dwarfs' dam on the Nile."

That did it.

Before I knew what was happening, we were surrounded by guards. They formed a tight ring around us. One guard put his sword against David's neck while another removed Galahad's sword from David's side. David, very wisely, didn't resist.

"Walk," the first guard commanded.

We did. Not much choice. We were led through the open courtyard and into Dagger-Mouth itself. If looks could kill . . . Word must have spread like wildfire throughout the place because every dwarf we passed glared and glowered at us.

"We are, officially, history," Christopher muttered. "Etain, I want you to take a good hard look at this bunch. Okay? That's all I'm saying."

She didn't answer.

Through a doorway, down a long, low-ceilinged, dimly lit corridor. Some of the guards had spurlike things on the heels of their boots, which clanged noisily on the metal flooring. Our own worn-down sneakers didn't make a sound.

We seemed to be descending slightly as we

made our way deeper into the castle. The grade wasn't dramatic but the muscles in my legs definitely told me we were penetrating slowly into the bowels of the earth.

Finally, the guards called a halt at a massive pair of double doors. Steel, of course, studded with more steel. One slipped inside the room beyond and we waited.

We didn't have to wait long. The doors were flung open from inside and we were summoned to enter by the guard who'd gone ahead.

With a little unnecessary shoving, the guards brought us into what I saw was a throne room. Where King Baldwin received visitors and, it seemed, prisoners.

I took a quick look around the room. No windows, which made me think we were indeed below the surface of the earth now. Small oil and coal lamps lined the walls at regular intervals. Each was lit but the room was too large to be fully brightened by anything less than electricity. Male and female dwarfs, though far fewer of the latter, stood in small groups around the room. Ladies and gentlemen of the court? As far as general proportion, the female dwarfs didn't look so different from the males.

There were also some male dwarfs who were dressed more finely than most and who clutched rolls of what might have been documents. Officers or advisers, I guessed. One thing was the same about every dwarf in the room. A scowling face.

Besides the lamps, which were really a necessity, there were no other decorations or embellishments. Except for the king, who sat on a large, austere steel throne. No cushions or velvet or footstool even.

King Baldwin wasn't really ugly. He was a bit taller than the average dwarf and a bit more nicely proportioned. Maybe this made him ugly to a dwarf's eyes but it made him almost attractive to a human's. His hair was chestnut brown and clean, by Everworld's standards. His face, too, was less stony, more animated than any I'd seen so far in DaggerMouth, with very large brown eyes and a great smile. Lots of teeth, very rakish, a perfectly styled goatee that added to his appeal. Baldwin emanated a definite mix of danger and devilry, seriousness and wit. I didn't want to like him, necessarily, not with his basically buying Etain in marriage, but somehow, I did.

Now I just had to hope he wouldn't kill us.

"Speak, human," Baldwin said now, nodding at David.

"I am David Levin, also known as General Davideus, in service to the goddess Athena. I am responsible for destroying your dam on the river Nile."

"You know," Christopher whispered, "that boy just has a way with words. He's just so — I don't know — so subtle."

Jalil gave Christopher a withering look.

King Baldwin looked amused in spite of himself.

"Yes, my guards have informed me," he said. "Allow me a moment to register your audacity in coming here and so boldly announcing your crime." Baldwin paused. "I will tell you that I have long awaited the day when I would meet those responsible for the destruction of our dam. And for the death of my cousin, Drogar. He died in the flames that engulfed the workers' sleeping quarters. From what I have been told, he did not have a chance to save himself. You understand, then, if I proceed to mete out the punishment you deserve for causing such horror."

I was scared. Not David. He didn't even try to apologize.

"Not before you hear me out. Hear us out. We are emissaries of Merlin the Magnificent."

"I know who he is," Baldwin grumbled, slightly chastened.

"And we bring you the Princess Etain of Merlinshire." David could barely restrain a sneer of distaste. None of us were fond of the idea of handing over women like chattel.

Christopher bristled. Etain stepped out from behind him.

"I bring myself, good King Baldwin. I ask you to pardon my rather disheveled appearance. I am here to offer myself in marriage to you, if you will still have me as your bride."

Baldwin frowned at each of us in turn but directed his next question to David. "Is this some sort of trick, human?"

"It's no trick," David replied. "What Etain says is true. She will marry you. But we want to make a deal first."

"Great King Baldwin, there are two conditions to my offer," Etain said, her voice firm.

"Speak, Princess Etain."

"First, my friends are not to be held prisoner or receive punishment for their previous actions against the dwarf kingdom."

Baldwin grumbled but the way he was looking at Etain, it was pretty clear he was seriously hot for her.

"Very well. Even a king is but a vassal to his wife. I will grant your first condition."

"I thank you humbly, good sir. My second condition is this. That you and your people form a true bond with Merlinshire — beyond even our marriage — by joining the military alliance of General Davideus, Merlin, and my good mother, Goewynne."

Baldwin said, "Why should I join this alliance? What is in it for me and my kingdom? What does King Camulos have to say to this proposal?"

Etain looked at David and he nodded. With his usual lack of ceremony and sugarcoating, David recounted the battle between Merlinshire and the Sennites, including the ignominious death of King Camulos.

"I am truly sorry to hear of the death of such a fine man," Baldwin said. "And of the suffering the princess and her good mother the queen have endured. But who are these Sennites with weapons so powerful? And why should I risk the welfare of my own kingdom to fight with you against them?"

David explained Senna. At least, that she was a witch who had been a gateway between worlds. That now she was dead, though her band of soldiers lived on. Christopher added an occasional caustic remark. Jalil added some of the details David chose to leave out. Like the fact that Senna had dragged us to Everworld with her. No one mentioned the fact that I had killed her.

"We're afraid the Sennites might try to unite

with Ka Anor and his Hetwan followers," David went on. "That's a deadly combination. No one in Everworld will be safe, gods or mortals. Weapons technology alone is a major problem. With a couple of mortars the Sennites could blow this castle apart before you'd have time to blink."

Baldwin thought about this.

"What is it you ask, exactly?" he finally demanded.

"Gold. Enough to hire all the fairy archers who will fight. And your own formidable troops. We want to stop the Sennites or Ka Anor, take out one force before they join up together. Then take out the other."

Baldwin considered.

"I agree. But I have a condition of my own. I will commit no more than one thousand bars of gold or their equivalent in silver to your cause." Baldwin smiled silkily at Etain. "A small enough consideration for the happiness the fair Etain will bring me and my kingdom."

I shot a glance at Christopher. He looked simultaneously sick and like he was going to fling himself at Baldwin's throat. I grabbed his elbow.

"One other thing," David said.

"He could have thanked the guy, first," Jalil muttered.

Baldwin frowned. "What is it?"

"We intend to rescue Thor. He's being held prisoner."

"Who dares to hold mighty Thor against his will?"

"Hel."

"Here it comes," Christopher whispered, calmer now. "The product has hit the fan."

"Are you mad?!" Baldwin thundered.

"Yup." Jalil said under his breath.

David went on as if he hadn't heard Baldwin's explosion. "We intend to cut a tunnel into Hel's domain. We need your help and expertise with this project. In one week Merlin will arrive with whatever help he's been able to muster, including Mjolnir, Thor's hammer. And Queen Goewynne will bring her people, the elves. That's the start of a serious army."

"And the end of my participation," Baldwin answered. "I am truly sorry, Princess Etain. But not even for your lovely hand in marriage will I risk infuriating Hel and so endangering my kingdom. I wish you success in your mad scheme, General Davideus. But I will not lend my support."

"Oh, yeah. That's true love," Christopher hissed.

"He's giving her up and you're complaining?" I said.

"Oh. Right. Just that he insulted her and all."

David wasn't finished. "Merlin helped form this plan. He believes it can work. You know he's not stupid."

"No, not stupid," Baldwin agreed. "But maybe desperate, and that is almost as bad."

Baldwin continued to protest but I saw something in his eye, some spark of interest. It was David's mention of Merlin's particular support.

"Enough discussion for now," Baldwin suddenly announced. "I keep my pledge to the fair Etain to treat you all as my guests. General Davideus, you may have your sword. Those of you who wish to retire for the night will be shown to your quarters. Those who wish to wander the Great Diggings first are welcome to do so."

Baldwin shook his head and stood. "I will retire to my private chambers to give this matter further consideration."

CHAPTER
XIV

Etain was led off by two dwarf women to what was no doubt the luxury suite. I didn't join David, Jalil, and Christopher on their before-bedtime tour of the Great Diggings. Wasn't in the mood for sight-seeing. All I wanted was to go to sleep, go back home, to my world, make sure I was still whole there, that Everworld April wasn't sucking the life — literally — out of real-world April.

I was shown to my room. It was no Hotel Olympus but neither was it a peasant's cottage complete with pigs, chickens, and competing colonies of lice. The dwarfs were solidly working-class, not outrageously rich but not desperately poor, either. The air might not have been the freshest and the light was dim at best, but in general things were clean and well-built. A bed, a chair, and a table, made of wood the dwarfs had probably traded for. On the table sat a basin and pitcher made of some sort of stone.

The female dwarf who'd brought me here left. After not acknowledging my thank you.

Wearily I picked up the sacklike gown she'd left for me to sleep in. It seemed luxurious compared to the filthy, bloodstained robes I had been wearing since the final battle at Merlinshire. Of course, the gown came to only just under my butt so it was really more of a skimpy nightshirt but I was happy to have it.

Gratefully, I stripped. Began to give myself a sponge bath at the large basin. God bless the clean, industrious, mind-their-own-business dwarfs. Even if they killed us later, they were offering me a bath and a bed now. Now was all that mattered.

Except, of course, for the hole in my chest.

I grabbed hold of the low bedpost to support myself. No mirror so I bent my head as far as my neck would stretch. Tentatively touched the place with my fingertip and sucked in a breath when my finger disappeared inside my body.

I couldn't see it perfectly, but oh, yes, there was a sort of hole, a hazy hole, like Jalil and like Christopher. Except my hole was forming in Everworld April.

Everworld April was fading away.

CHAPTER
XV

Asleep in Everworld.

Magda, Becka, Tyra, and me. Blind Faith cafe. After school. Stopping by for a quick snack before taking in the new Russell Crowe movie at the Cineplex. Everyone ordered the usual. Everyone sat in her usual place. It could have been any one of the hundreds of times we'd been here, catching some food before catching a movie.

The waiter went off to get our orders.

I listened to my friends but heard only part of what they were saying. Or maybe it was the other way around. I heard their familiar voices, laughing and chattering in the familiar tones, but did I actually listen to what it was they were laughing and chattering about? Suddenly, it seemed to require a big effort to focus on the words and their meanings.

I felt like maybe this was what it was like to be drunk or high. Or maybe this was just boredom. That disturbed me.

"He is fine, that boy." Magda's voice.

"Girl, you are deficient! He's got a nose the size of Detroit!"

"Yeah, but you know what they say about a big nose. Big nose, big . . ."

"Box of tissues."

Howls of laughter. I smiled. It was funny.

But the silly joke didn't make me forget my other life, the life that since Senna's death seemed more important and vital and essential than it ever had.

It was getting progressively harder for real-world April to keep Everworld at bay. I suspected also that real-world April was not trying as hard as she once did to keep both worlds apart.

Even sitting with good friends, people with whom I'd lived so much of my life, people who loved me and kept me safe, I couldn't ignore the fact that David was still missing here in the real world.

Rumors had begun to sprout and spread. The usual outlandish stuff, like he'd joined a cult, and the less crazy, like he'd heard from Senna and gone off to join her. Of course, there was fear, too. Maybe he'd been murdered by some psycho killer of high school kids. Ten years from now the cops would find his body and Senna's and probably others in a ditch on the outskirts of town.

I knew no one would ever find David or his body. I knew that he was alive and well but in some other world. Keeping that enormous secret was — strange.

It was strange, too, to keep silent in the real world about all the other people who had become so important to me. People whose lives affected mine so closely. Like, I couldn't forget Etain's dilemma. Forced to marry a man she didn't love, compelled by duty to reject the man she did, all for the good of her people. Etain was making an enormous personal sacrifice and I so wished I could help her somehow. So wished I could help Christopher accept what Etain was doing, respect her wishes, so wished I could ease his pain. Because it was genuine, I could see that.

I wished I could help myself, too. Everworld April was slipping away and why why why was that worrying me? It was what I'd always wanted, to leave Everworld for good. But now that it looked like that might be happening, I . . . I didn't know what I wanted.

And I so couldn't forget that final moment with Senna. What had happened inside me at that moment to give me the strength to kill her?

I felt sure I could never do it again, if somehow Senna had survived, which I also knew was impossible. I felt sure I never could have premeditated her death. If only . . . If only what?

"April, you with us?"

"Huh? Oh, yeah, sorry. I was just thinking." I smiled. I really didn't want my friends to think anything was wrong with me. With us.

Becka shook her head. "Too much thinking is a bad thing, April, you know that. You sure you're okay?"

"Yeah," Tyra said, "lately you seem, I don't know, like you're someplace else. Not all the time but a lot of the time."

Magda leaned forward. "You know you can count on us, girl. Something going on at home? That creepy half sister of yours didn't show up again, did she?"

Becka pretended to shiver. "Evil."

"No, no," I said. "Everything's cool, really. Nothing's going on."

"Okay, if you say so."

"Just let us know if something is going on, all right?"

The conversation swerved away from me. I put my hands in my lap and squeezed them together. No, Senna wouldn't be showing up again.

I looked around, over my shoulder.

I spotted Jalil and was suddenly happy. He was sitting tall, back very straight. Looked odd. He gestured to me with his head.

"Be back in a minute," I said to my friends. Tyra gave me a strange look. I got up and made my way through the crowded cafe, to the small table at the back where Jalil sat. A cup of coffee, untouched, and a scone, one bite gone, sat before him. His hands were in his lap. His face was impassive.

"Hi," I said.

"Sit in front of me. Your back to the cafe," Jalil instructed, a false smile on his face, like he was saying, "Hey, April, good to see you!"

I did as he instructed. Shook my head like, "What?" Said, "I feel like I'm in some gangster movie. Or *The Sopranos*. Who are you hiding from?"

"Don't react or anything, okay?"

I nodded.

"Good. I'm sitting here, waiting for Miyuki. I take a bite of that scone, chew, think I'll take a sip of coffee, wash it down. That's when I realize, my hand, the one reaching for the cup, it's gone. I mean, suddenly, it's just not there. So I put it in my lap and presto, there it is again. Only before it gets solid, it kind of flickers into view. Nothing, flicker, hand. Keeps happening."

This was not good.

"Jalil, you've got to get out of here before Miyuki shows up. What if she sees? I'll tell her you didn't feel well and went home, something. Stick your hands in your pockets, get up, walk out. Did you pay? I'll pay for you, just go."

Jalil smiled wanly. "And what's that going to do? Sooner or later I'm going to have to take my hands out of my pockets, like to, I don't know, open a door, and someone's going to notice. Someone's going to say, 'Gee, that young man has translucent hands. Interesting effect.' April, something's got to happen. Soon. I can't live this way here. It won't work. I think I'm being kicked out of my life."

I leaned forward.

"Or you're choosing to go. Jalil, I think I know what's going on. I think we have to choose, one world or another. You, you're not so attached to this life, the real world, anymore. Neither is Christopher. That's why you're both fading away. Not completely, and if you don't choose you'll continue to flicker in and out. But David, from the beginning he's wanted out of this world, wanted to stay in Everworld. He's got a purpose there, or at least he feels he does. That's why he's gone here, totally. He made the commitment to Everworld."

"And you, April?"

"Me, I . . . I'm still whole here. But Everworld April, Jalil, she's fading. Look, I've never wanted to stay there. I've always wanted things to go back to the way they were before. Before Senna dragged us down to the lake."

"And now? You know it'll never be like it was. You can't go back, pretend Everworld never happened."

"I know. And it freaks me out to admit this, but I'm not thrilled Everworld April is fading out. I . . . I just don't know what I want. I'm not ready to choose."

"I don't feel like I'm choosing," Jalil said.

"But you are. You must be."

"Damn. There's Miyuki.

"Do you want me to stay?" I said.

Jalil smiled. "No, but thanks. If I'm on my way out of here, I want to spend as much time with my new girlfriend as I can. Alone. Even with see-through hands."

I stood up from the table, knees weak. And then I woke up to pounding.

Everworld. Pound, pound, pound.

BAM. BAM. BAM.

"What?" I opened my eyes. It took a second to realize where I was but it always did, waking up in Everworld. Low-ceilinged room, rock walls, rough-but-sturdy wood furniture, a large stone basin, and a pitcher of water. My room in Dag-gerMouth. I stumbled out of the too-short bed in my too-short nightshirt. Saw that during the night someone had brought me fresh clothing and taken my filthy robes to be washed. Or burned.

"Who is it?"

"It's me, Christopher. Open up."

I unlatched the thick steel door and yanked it open. "Oof. This door weighs a ton," I complained.

"It feels heavier because you're still half asleep," Christopher said, brushing past me.

"Oh? And whose fault is that?"

He didn't answer, just flung himself full length on my rumpled bed. I sat down at the foot, where his knees were.

My eyes traveled up to Christopher's face. His eyes were troubled. He rubbed his face with his hands and sighed.

"What am I gonna do? I mean, she won't even talk to me."

"I assume you're talking about Etain?"

He didn't respond. No funny comment. No insult. I don't even think he heard me. He hadn't even leered at my naked legs.

The boy had it bad.

"I've hardly seen her since we got to Dagger-Mouth," he went on, "what with her being a princess and all, a special guest. And then when I do run into her she's surrounded by all these dwarf women. Maybe it's their fault. Maybe they won't let her talk to me. Etain turns away, but maybe she's just obeying orders because she has no choice. . . ."

"Just forget her, Christopher." Maybe I sounded cranky or harsh. I mean, he'd woken me up. I yawned. "There's still a good chance she's going to have to marry Baldwin. You'll just have to move on."

Christopher looked at me like he was disappointed. Like he'd thought he was talking to someone named April but had just discovered he'd been talking to someone named Fred.

"You know, April," he said. "It doesn't work that way. It's just not that easy. Man, I thought I'd never hear myself say this, but I'm in love with Etain. I love her. Have you ever been in love? Do you even have a clue what it feels like? And I don't even have a fair shot with her. I don't even get to date her and drive her crazy with my stupid TV obsession and have her give me the big Ultimato — that she wants to get married now or she's moving on. I don't get to buy her a ring and get down on my knees and make a fool of myself asking her to be my wife. I don't get to hold her hand while she's delivering our baby. I don't get to show her off at office Christmas parties. . . ."

"There are no office Christmas parties in Everworld," I pointed out. "At least not the kind you mean. Shrimp on ice and lots of free booze and people making Xerox copies of their butts."

"Don't you care about her at all?" he said angrily.

"Look, it's not about Etain. I mean, of course I

care, I like her, I admire her. But I'm thinking about you. Senna's . . . death left us sort of flickering between the real world and Everworld. The more attached you become to Everworld, the less you're around in the real world. Look at David. He's gone over there, just gone. You and Jalil, you're fading away back home. You know why you stop fading when you get into a TV show? Because TV anchors you, it's so uniquely real world, it holds you down, keeps you from floating away. Christopher, if you get too involved here, you'll lose the real world."

Christopher sat up and leaned toward me. His tone was urgent.

"Would that be so awful, April? What would I be giving up, huh? Two drunk parents. An obnoxious little brother. A future all mapped out for a guy like me: middle management, an affair that breaks up my marriage, kids who become druggies, bald by the time I'm fifty, a heart attack by the time I'm fifty-five. Prostate cancer by my late sixties. You know, the usual suburban scenario for the average American male. Here's the worst of it. I used to think that all would be okay. I'm a simple guy, April, never wanted much. Always thought I'd be content to slide by, have some laughs along the way. Man, I used to rag David, we all did, about his bitter vision of adulthood.

Now, well, I'm no wanna-be hero type like David, but now that life just doesn't seem right."

I had no argument to make. Just a warning for a friend.

"If you stay here, Christopher, you could still lose Etain. Nothing's going to change Baldwin's mind if he decides to go through with the deal."

"Maybe." He nodded, thoughtful. "But maybe that's a chance I have to take. Maybe if I have to live out the rest of my life without Etain, it's better I do it here. At least there'll be plenty of mind-blowing action to take my mind off my pain."

Suddenly, the comedian Christopher, trying to make the grief bearable. "Maybe I'll even die a glorious death before my time. Die young and leave a good-looking corpse. That would be something. Wouldn't it?"

CHAPTER
XVII

We were summoned to a meal. Breakfast, I figured, though there wasn't a bowl of Shredded Wheat or a glass of orange juice in sight. David, Jalil, Christopher, and me. Etain, a royal visitor, was probably eating with the king and his court.

Dark bread, meat stew, mushrooms. The entire meal was brown, including the ale and some other liquid that was supposed to be water. The meat was not bat — I asked — but I stuck to the bread and mushrooms.

David ate silently and swiftly, his sword buckled at his side. Jalil spooned food into his mouth with one hand and made notes and sketches on a large sheet of thick, cream-colored paper with the other.

Christopher had arranged one of every variety

of mushroom in a circle on his plate. Fifteen mushrooms. It was a very large plate.

"There's a fungus among us," he muttered. I didn't laugh. He sighed. "Look, I am trying to be lighthearted over here. The least you can do is pretend to laugh. Okay? The woman I love is still in danger of being married off. I'm not in top form."

"Baldwin is a king," I pointed out.

"He's a freakin' dwarf."

"He does seem nice. Not mean and all. You should be glad about that, anyway. For Etain's sake."

"Look, April, I'm not all moral and noble like you, okay? I'm a dog. I'm self-centered and of course I want Etain to be happy no matter what she decides to do with her life. But more than that I want me to be happy, with her, okay? End of story."

"I'm sorry. I want you to be happy, too. With Etain."

His smile was wobbly. "Thanks."

When we'd eaten all the earthy fare we could stomach, we were summoned to the throne room where we'd first met King Baldwin. He was going to give us his final decision. One look at his face, all grim and sober, and we knew what he was going to say.

"I am sorry. But I will not endanger the Great Diggings, my people, and my kingdom, by invading Hel's domain. I deeply regret the loss of Princess Etain as my wife. And I appreciate the sacrifice she was prepared to make for her own people. I wish I could accept her noble gift but I cannot."

"Wait." Jalil. "King Baldwin, please, I have something to show you."

Baldwin smiled wearily. "Is it great enough to change the royal ruling on this matter?"

Jalil nodded. "Yes. I think it is."

Baldwin was taken by surprise. "Very well, then, approach."

Add "tolerant" to a list of Baldwin's good features.

Jalil pulled a roll of what turned out to be drawings from his shirt and brought them up to the king.

"I spent some time looking around your operation. You're doing okay, but you could be doing a lot better."

Baldwin looked momentarily annoyed but nodded for Jalil to go on.

"One: You've got plenty of coal, no problem there. But you're not using it efficiently. I mean, you could be doing a lot more with it. You know King Camulos had electricity in his castle, right?

Well, you can have it here, too, in DaggerMouth. I can build you a coal-fired electrical plant, light up everything. The tunnels, the workshops. You can have instant communication throughout the Great Diggings. Okay? Telegraph, first. No more hand-delivered notes. Better than that, I can build you a train, like one in Merlinshire, to carry the ore up from the mines in a fraction of the time it takes you now. Your entire mining enterprise will be two, three times more productive. That means more gold. Lots of gold. And I haven't even gotten to the possibility of automating some of your manufacturing work. That's down the line but it can happen."

Baldwin was sitting forward in his throne, hands on his knees. The guy was hooked.

Christopher's face was dark. "What the hell is Jalil doing?" he hissed. "He's basically throwing my girlfriend at this guy. . . ."

"Continue," Baldwin commanded.

"Here's the deal. I gave the fairies the telegraph. They transferred the technology to Merlinshire. Now they've got electricity. But neither the fairies nor the Irish humans have the dwarfs' skill. There are hundreds, thousands of ways your kingdom can benefit from electricity. You can use it to push more fresh air into the deep wells or to pump water out. Look, from what I can tell you've almost reached the limit of your mining capabilities. I give you electricity, there are no limits."

"No limits," Baldwin repeated in a low voice.

"No limits," Jalil confirmed.

Baldwin paused for a moment before speaking. "I believe, perhaps, I made a hasty decision when I refused to support your raid on Hel. I have changed my mind. I will risk Hel's enmity and commit my kingdom to the fight against the Sennites and that foul beast Ka Anor. My conditions are these: You . . ."

"Jalil."

"Strange name, but you, *Jalil*, you will commence work directly on the first stage of your plan to introduce electricity to the Great Diggings. In the meantime, my men will begin construction of the tunnel to Hel. It will be ready by the time Merlin arrives with his magic and Queen Goewynne with her reinforcements. General Davideus will supervise."

Baldwin now rose from his throne and turned to face Etain, standing with a small group of female dwarf.

"Fair Etain," he began, "does your offer of marriage still stand? For it is the second of my conditions for this treaty."

"It does, good sir," Etain answered.

Baldwin held out his hand and Etain came forward to take it. Together they faced the room, Etain standing on the floor, Baldwin on the step to his throne, almost the same height this way.

"May I present to you your future queen!" Baldwin cried out.

I turned to look for Christopher but he was gone.

CHAPTER
XVIII

Real-world April went to church but I left without going to confession. Without receiving the Sacrament of Reconciliation, as it's now called. When I got home there was an undercover police car in the driveway. I wondered if anyone is ever fooled by an undercover police car. They all look alike: bland-colored sedans, no trim, nothing to make them stand out, which, of course, makes them stand out.

I walked up the drive, breathing the cold evening air. *This is it, April,* I told myself. It's time for the greatest role of your life. Time for you to play innocent high school junior, still utterly puzzled about the several-month disappearance of her half sister. Sad but recovering, moving on.

It shouldn't be too hard, I thought. My parents and I had been feigning concern since Senna left home. We'd been deceiving the world and one another. What was one more harmless deception on my part? *No, officer, I have no idea where Senna is right now. I haven't seen her since she left home. Why, do you have a lead?*

But the police weren't there to talk about Senna, at least not at first.

My parents were sitting on the living room couch, very close, shoulders touching. When I got to the door of the room, my father stood and said in his gentle voice, "April, honey, these police officers need to talk to you about one of your classmates." Then he sat back down.

I stepped into the room and glanced wide-eyed at the two plainclothes detectives who stood in front of the fireplace. One held a small notebook and pen. They each wore a slightly rumpled but clean sports jacket, button-down shirt and slacks. Sears catalog. Nondescript.

"Okay," I said. I joined my parents on the couch, perched on the edge of the cushion. Give them nothing, let them ask the questions, April. Already I was thinking like a criminal.

"I'm Detective Costello and this is Detective Hayes, Miss O'Brien. Do you know a boy named David Levin?" Detective Costello asked. The talker. The other one would take the notes.

"Yes," I said simply.

"How well do you know him?"

I shrugged. "Not well. He goes to my school."

"Is that all?"

I pretended to think. "He's in my grade."

"Didn't he date your sister for a while, before she disappeared?"

Well, duh, certainly not after she disappeared, I thought. *Careful, April.*

"I think so. I mean, I heard they were seeing each other. Senna was very private."

"*Was* private?" There was a gleam in Detective Costello's eye.

"Yes," I said. "When she was living here, at home. She was private."

"So you weren't close to your sister, Miss O'Brien?"

"My half sister," I said. "No, we weren't very close."

My mother put her hand on my arm, reassuringly.

"Are you aware, Miss O'Brien, that David Levin has not been at school all week?"

Careful again, April. They might know you spoke to his mother. And why would you do that if you didn't know him very well?

"I heard he was out," I said carefully. "From my best friend. She's doing a social studies project with him; he's her assigned partner. She was upset he wasn't at school to help."

"Is that why you called his house and spoke to Mrs. Levin?"

Oh, crap, it was going to sound lame but it was the best I could do at the moment. Especially with cold sweat suddenly cascading down my back.

"Yes. I mean, first my friend called but Mrs. Levin didn't really say if David was home. So I called, too. To help out my friend."

Detective Costello didn't buy my story for a second. I could see the disbelief all over his face. Even I'd heard the falseness in my voice.

"Miss O'Brien, is it usual for you to interfere —"

"Detective Costello." My mother. "My daughter and her girlfriends are very close. It is not at all unusual for them to help one another with their school work or drama club projects."

Detective Costello held up his hand as if to acquiesce, then shot me a look. My mother's defense had shut him up, but he still knew I was lying. And he wanted me to know he knew.

"Miss O'Brien," he continued, "what did Mrs. Levin tell you when you spoke with her?"

I pretended to think hard. "I think she said something about David not being home. Something about not having seen him around the house."

"Miss O'Brien, when was the last time you saw David Levin?"

Here, in the real world, you mean? "Uh, I don't remember, exactly. Sometime last week, I guess. Maybe in the cafeteria?"

My father cleared his throat. "Look, officers, I really don't see the point in your asking my daughter all these questions. She says she hardly knows the boy. And my wife and I can tell you that if this David Levin was involved with our daughter Senna, we didn't know about it. Senna never brought any boy home. She was very independent."

Suddenly, I thought I was going to cry. I was doing a lot of crying these days. But I was immensely grateful for my parents' support. And immensely guilty about it, too.

Detective Hayes closed his notebook and nodded at his partner.

"Mr. O'Brien, let me be blunt."

Detective Costello stuck his hands in his pants pockets. I noticed the material was a little saggy. "I think your daughter knows more than she's telling us. About David Levin and Senna Wales."

I continued to stare at his pockets. This man was smarter than he looked. But my father believed me. He believed his daughter was telling the truth. Why shouldn't he, when to his knowledge she'd never given him reason to distrust her.

"Detective Costello, my daughter is an honor student and an active member of our church. She's the last person to lie, especially about something as important as a missing classmate, and especially not to the police. Now, gentlemen, I'm asking you to leave our home."

They did. But not without pressing the point that if I suddenly remembered anything, anything at all about either Senna or David, any little incident that might help the police in their investigation, I was to contact Detective Costello immediately.

I said, "Of course, officers, I will."

"Mrs. Levin is a single parent," Detective Costello explained as he stood in the doorway. Night had fallen. "David is her only child. She's very concerned. You'll keep that in mind, won't you?"

"I will," I promised.

CHAPTER XIX

When the police left, my mother asked me what I wanted for dinner. As if I deserved a treat after my ordeal.

"How about I go pick up some Thai food?" my father suggested. "We'll have a nice dinner together, try to forget that unpleasantness. What do you say?"

My mother just nodded. She looked very tired.

I said, "I'm sorry, Dad. I'm going out tonight. I already made plans."

He was disappointed. And I got the feeling that maybe he didn't want to be alone with my mother right now. After all, Senna was his daughter, not hers, and all Senna had ever done was cause trouble. Even now, months after Senna had left, my mother was still dealing with police coming into her home and questioning her own daughter, the legitimate product of a lawful marriage, about Senna Wales, illegitimate result of my father's affair.

But tonight I wouldn't be the buffer zone. Tonight they would have to do without me.

I had a date. His name was Trey and I'd met him at the Rave Cafe the week before while waiting for Magda to show up. He asked if he could share a table and I said, sure, but only until my friend came. We talked. He was twenty-one years old and a senior at the university. He was planning to go to business school for an MBA. At one point my cell phone rang. Magda was still at the doctor's office. The doctor was running late. I said, no problem, I'll see you tomorrow in school. Then Trey asked me out, for dinner at one of the hottest restaurants in town. I hadn't been there before. It wasn't the sort of place you went with your parents, and my friends and I had decided we probably wouldn't fit in with the crowd, mostly twenty-somethings, being only high school juniors.

I'd said sure, and that I'd meet him there. He didn't offer to pick me up, which I appreciated. I hadn't lied about my age. He had to be relieved not to have to meet my parents.

Okay, this was a bold move. A date with an older guy, a guy about to graduate college in a few months, a guy who was into business and not the theater, that was huge. A date I hadn't gone into specifics with parents about because they'd never have let me go, and I'd really wanted to. Not that I was in love with Trey or anything, I'd only talked with him for an hour, but . . . Well, I'm not sure why, exactly, but somehow it seemed important to meet him for dinner. I wanted the experience to be all mine. I just didn't want to have to report every detail of the date to Magda and Becka and the others. I wanted to live it and then remember it, figure it out on my own, make my own decision about Trey.

It's just a date, April, I told myself as I finished getting dressed. But I knew it was more than that.

I asked to borrow my dad's car and he said okay. What trouble could his honor student, churchgoing daughter get into?

I parked a block away from the restaurant. Il Panino. I was a bit early, not too much. I pulled open the door to Il Panino and walked purposefully to the hostess. She was slim and tall and dressed all in black.

"Hi, I'm meeting someone here at seven," I said.

"Great. Do you see him?"

The place was small. I glanced around.

"No."

"Okay then, would you like to wait at the bar?"

"Sure." I smiled a sophisticated smile.

I was in.

CHAPTER
XX

Trey was three minutes late. Not that I was counting. We were shown to a small round table against an exposed brick wall. On the wall was a painting of a fig. A label listed the price as three hundred and fifty dollars. The fig was pink.

We ordered appetizers and a bottle of sparkling water. Lime for me, lemon for Trey. He looked great, even older than twenty-one. I'm pretty sure his jacket was Armani or a very good knockoff. We ate bruschetta and talked easily. It was turning out to be a pretty good date.

Until about halfway through the main course.

"Oh . . . oh, my god, April?"

Trey scooted his chair away from the table. The legs made a loud and unpleasant noise on the tiled floor.

"What? What's wrong?" I said. One minute

we're having a decent conversation. The next minute he's looking at me like I'm some freak show reject. His eyes were wide, mouth opened, throat working.

"Do I have something in my teeth, what?"

Trey put his hand to his forehead. "I think maybe I'm sick. Or something. You, your face . . ."

I knew. I touched my cheek anyway. My fingers met air.

"Oh, God, you just, it's not me! You're, like, fading or something!"

Trey looked like he really might be sick. By now people at the other tables were watching us. I grabbed my bag and mumbled, "I'm sorry, I have to go."

And I ran, head down, out to the street. Tore down the block to my car, fumbled wildly for the keys, then locked myself in and flipped down the visor on the passenger side. Looked into the mirror there.

Half a face looked back at me. A flickering and my left eye returned, went away, came back again.

I watched, fascinated, until my entire face came back into view. Then I leaned my head against the steering wheel.

It was finally happening. Real-world April was leaving home.

After a minute I started the car and began to drive toward Christopher's house. I needed to tell him it was finally happening to me. Then I would look for Jalil.

It didn't, of course, occur to me to go home. Or to call Magda. I needed to talk without having to lie.

I drove to Christopher's house. A block away I saw flashing lights and knew they were for him. I parked a few houses down, ran past the faces peeping curiously from windows and the nosy woman standing in an open doorway, mouth gaping.

One ambulance, one police car. Great. The way my day was going, Detectives Costello and Hayes would come cruising around the corner next.

Just as I reached the Hitchcocks' lawn, the front door opened. Two paramedics wheeled a gurney over the doorsill and lifted it down the few stairs to the front walk. Christopher's father stood in the open door and watched his son being wheeled away.

"Christopher!" I raced to his side and gripped the metal edge of the gurney. Walked along with the paramedics, who seemed strangely disturbed and nervous. "What happened?"

"Boys, how about you let me talk to my friend here for a minute, okay?"

The paramedics stopped wheeling. *Since when is a patient in charge,* I thought.

Christopher didn't look sick. In fact, he looked kind of — happy. "Well, April, Mom caught a glimpse of me without my shirt on. Didn't know she'd come into my room to put away some laundry."

"You mean . . ."

"Take a look." Christopher yanked the sheet covering him from the leather restraints. The paramedics stepped back.

I sucked in a breath. "I see. Or, I don't see. Whatever."

Christopher was mostly not there. No chest, but some stomach. One shoulder.

He leered. "Want to see what else is missing?"

"No. Oh, my god, Christopher." I leaned close to his ear. "How are you going to explain this? What are you going to do?!"

"Keep my mouth shut," he said. "What else can I do? And you're looking a little, uh, pale, too, right now. If you know what I mean."

"I started to fade out at dinner. I was on a date and the guy freaked. I came right over to see you."

"Yeah, well, thanks. I guess. Look, I suggest you get home, now. Go in the back way, don't let your mother see you. Or we're gonna be roomies in intensive care."

"Okay. Christopher, the police came to my house today," I said in a rush. "They wanted to know about Senna and David. They know I'm not telling the truth. I . . ."

"Don't wait up for me, April," Christopher said, as if he hadn't heard me at all, a strange, spacey smile on his face. "I think you might be wasting your time."

The paramedics had snapped back into professional mode. Maybe because Mr. Hitchcock was shouting at them to get the hell to the hospital. "Please step back, miss," one said.

I did. He replaced the sheet over Christopher, but not before letting his hand slide into the nothingness. Then the paramedics hoisted the gurney up and into the back of the ambulance.

"Christopher, I want to go with you," I said.

"Only family, please," the stocky paramedic told me and helped Christopher's mother into the back with her son. When she passed close to me I thought I smelled alcohol.

"April, I . . ."

I didn't hear what Christopher was about to say. The stocky paramedic slammed the doors shut and locked them into place.

I stood and watched as Christopher was sped off to the emergency room. I stood and watched until the ambulance was out of sight.

Then I decided I'd go see Jalil.

And then I was in Everworld.

XXI

DaggerMouth, the Great Diggings, the Five Hills, King Baldwin's realm. A fairly awful subterranean kingdom, with little fresh air and less natural light, where for some reason I didn't mind so much being at the moment.

Until David asked me to go with him and Christopher to check the progress on the tunnel. Up to that point, I'd avoided the construction site, for the obvious reason. My intelligent brain knew it was unlikely, but my primitive brain couldn't help but picture Hel roaring up through the tunnel from her pit of misery and snatching me away. Like when you're a kid and someone tells you snakes can come up through the toilet and bite you. But far, far worse.

"Why do I have to go?" I asked.

"Jalil's too busy playing master engineer. I need

someone to keep Christopher in line. He doesn't listen to me."

"What are you afraid he's going to do?" I said.

David frowned. "Ruin everything, destroy the whole plan. He's determined that Etain won't marry Baldwin. If he freaks and tries to do something like kidnap her, everything is screwed."

"And you really think he'll listen to me?" I asked.

"Yeah. I do."

I couldn't decide whether I was pleased about David's confidence in me or just mad he was guilting me into exploring a tunnel that was a direct road to Hel.

Literally.

We started out at the main area of the work site, where the foreman was stationed and where small, portable tables were set up for the workers' on-the-job meals. Piles of pickaxes and shovels and coal-powered drills.

From there we progressed to the opening of the tunnel. The tunnel was low-ceilinged, high enough for me to walk without stooping but a bit tight for Christopher. And probably for Jalil, I guessed. The stone walls were slick with condensation. The air was thick and humid. The light was dim, provided by coal lamps hung along the walls every few feet. But the dwarfs had done a good job of clearing away loose rubble and any obstructing stones so walking wasn't really a problem. And the incline was gentle enough to prevent undo strain on the knees. The dwarfs definitely knew what they were doing.

Christopher was beyond grim. He was wound so tight it was like he could whirl his way through the floor of the tunnel like a drill. David kept his sword in its scabbard but his hand on the hilt.

I walked a bit behind both guys and wondered if I should tell them that I was fading now in the real world. I'd told real-world Christopher but as far as I could tell, Everworld Christopher knew nothing. The two people hadn't yet met again. Maybe they never would.

"Christopher, I think you're gone now in the real world," I said. "Or just about gone. You were taken by paramedics to the emergency room. I wanted to go with you but then I was back here. I don't know what real-world April is doing now."

Christopher looked at me over his shoulder and barked a laugh. "Those guys must be sick of hauling me off only to have the doctors throw up their hands in confusion and send me home. Maybe they think I'm faking it."

I shook my head. "Trust me, Christopher, there's no way you could be faking this. You were only half there, maybe only a quarter there, on the stretcher."

"Invisible paint?"

"Nope. One paramedic stuck his hand right through you."

"Hmmm. Maybe I'll be famous." He shrugged.

"You won't be around long enough to be famous," I said. "At this rate you'll be all gone in a day or two."

"Not a problem," he muttered, pushing his damp hair off his face. The humidity was beginning to be unbearable. "By the way," he asked me, "what happened to your idea about talking to Brigid? You know, to see if she could stop us from disappearing back there."

I nearly stopped walking. I'd forgotten all about my plan. And that was strange because I'd so hoped Brigid could help us.

"I just haven't had the time," I lied. "You know, I do lead a very busy life back home. Not quite as glamorous as my life here but . . ."

David looked at me with a look that said, "Oh, so it's finally happening to you, too. About time."

But I wasn't one hundred percent ready to join David's accept-the-inevitability-of-Everworld club. I was glad now I hadn't mentioned that real-world April was fading.

"Next time I go back," I said, "I'll go see her."
We walked.

Once Jalil had said he thought the real-world versions of us were becoming the subset. That the more that happened to us, the more we experienced in Everworld, the smaller our "real" lives were becoming. I was so angry with him then. I was angry because I knew he was telling the truth.

Now, here we were, the four of us, planning an invasion of Hel's domain, fading or already gone in the real world, more than likely we'd spend the rest of our lives in Everworld, a place of massive uncertainty, fear, and violence. And on some distant level, I really didn't mind.

The tunnel was almost finished. According to the foreman, a burly guy named Mergon, work would be over that evening. Right on schedule.

"I wonder if these guys are in a union?" Christopher asked, watching one of the workers collapse against a wall in exhaustion.

Then Mergon showed us a feature of the construction that made me simultaneously nervous and thankful. The dwarfs had prepared a safeguard. A thousand tons of slag and rock were being held suspended behind a breakaway barrier. Once we'd made it out of there with Thor and Baldur, the barrier would be knocked down and the tons of stone would seal the tunnel permanently.

Keeping Hel out of the Great Diggings. Maybe locking us out, too, if things didn't go as planned.

"So, uh, who's, you know, going in?" Christopher asked when Mergon had returned to supervising the final stages of construction.

"Jalil's got to stay with Baldwin and his crew. He's their prize; they won't risk losing him."

Christopher sighed dramatically. "So, it's you and me, David. Alone again. Naturally."

I kept my mouth shut. No one was even suggesting I go on the mission. Maybe because I was a girl and the stuff we'd seen in Hel was so brutally disgusting David was being manly and trying to protect me from it. Which didn't entirely make sense because as a woman I was somewhat immune to Hel's "charms."

"What about me?" I protested.

"We need only two people for this mission," David said. "No point in risking more lives."

"I'm going." I insisted. "You guys are going to need someone to haul your sorry butts out of there when she gives you the eye."

David didn't look convinced. "I can't stop you."

I grinned. And I'm not quite sure why.

CHAPTER
XXIII

A knock at the door. David's voice. We'd gone back to our rooms to get some rest before our big day. "Let's go, April."

"I'm coming," I called. I pulled the tunic back over my head, belted it up. Wished we still had Excalibur, that it was in my belt right now. But after I'd used it to kill Senna, I'd dropped it. No one had chosen to retrieve the knife.

I opened the door and joined David. Christopher was there, too. Silently we began the long walk to the opening of the tunnel.

We reached the construction site.

And that's when the panic hit. The bowel-loosening, stomach rumbling, cold-sweat panic that overcomes you when you realize you've done something very, very stupid.

Nothing good could come of this mission.

Nothing except that maybe Hel would scare me out of preferring Everworld to the nice, normal comforts and challenges of the real world. All my earlier bravado, gone. Now I was just a mass of quivering fear and doubt.

I stumbled aside and threw up. Felt my entire body convulse and shiver. Felt sweat trickle down from my hairline.

When the nausea had passed, I wiped my mouth with the hem of my tunic and turned back toward the others.

And saw that Jalil had joined us. So had Etain. I was sure I looked awful, hair all damp, face pale. Etain, on the other hand, looked lovely. Tired and sad, but as pretty as ever, her honest, wide-open charm undaunted by the grim reality around her.

"Etain's come to see us off," Christopher said with false gaiety. She seemed unable to meet his eye.

"Thanks," I said. "But it's probably not safe. . . ."

Uh. Can you say "understatement"?

"I have come to bring you this," she said, and held out a sword. It looked familiar. "It is my own," she explained. "An elfin sword, enchanted, of course. I have had it with me since Merlinshire." She smiled apologetically. "My secret protection, should the need arise. Now you, April, have far more need of it than I."

I didn't know what to say. "Thank you" seemed so lame. I reached out and Etain placed the sword in my hands. "This . . ." I began. "Thank you, Etain. This means so much to me." I slid the sword into my belt.

"You have become almost like a sister to me, April," Etain said, her voice full of emotion. Then she turned to look at David and, finally, Christopher.

"My thoughts are with each of you. May you return safely to DaggerMouth and to the friends who need you."

"That's the plan," Christopher said. I swear there were tears in his eyes.

"If Merlin arrives," David said, "while we're down there . . ."

"I will tell him to follow," Etain assured him. "And should my mother arrive with an army of elves . . ."

"I don't know what to tell you," David replied honestly. "We won't be able to communicate with you. I don't want elves sent in if it's too late. No point in wasting more lives."

Etain nodded. "I will speak to Merlin or King Baldwin for advice."

Nervously, we waited for the workers to push

through the final barrier of rock and dirt separating the dwarf kingdom from Hel's. Nobody said much of anything.

Baldwin had suggested we enter Hel's domain mounted. It would give us some small advantage, he said, particularly if — when — we had to run. I was more than sure there would be running involved.

Baldwin had sent an emissary to a neighboring aboveground village that prided themselves on their horseflesh. Whatever offer Baldwin made was accepted and now five sturdy mares were led toward us. One for each of us and one each for Thor and Baldur. No one assumed the two gods would be in any condition to stand and fight.

The horses were blindfolded in an effort to keep them from panicking in the subterranean world. Personally, I wasn't convinced the blindfolds were doing the trick. The horses were nervous, tossing their heads, snuffling, their chests and flanks slicked with sweat. Still, it was obvious they were well-trained because not one of them bolted. Which was good because the notion of riding helmets was unknown to the dwarfs. And none of us was exactly a jockey or professional polo player.

Baldwin had suggested another precaution, this one against the stench of death that would swarm out at us the moment the dwarf workers broke through. As sick as the smell would make us, it would drive the horses crazy. So each horse wore a small but fragrant bouquet of flowers and spicy herbs tied to its bridle, close to its nose.

Dwarfs are nothing if not reliable. At exactly the agreed-upon time, David, Christopher, and I were ready to begin our descent. Baldwin had not come to see us off. I suppose it wasn't smart for a king to get too close to the front lines of a too-dangerous mission. Etain murmured some sort of blessing and turned away quickly. Her new constant companions, two dwarf ladies-in-waiting, followed her off.

Mergon nodded in a manly way to David. David nodded back. Then Mergon handed Christopher a dwarf sword. Christopher took it with a sickly smile but said, "Thanks. I have a feeling I'm going to need this."

Jalil shook David's hand, then Christopher's. I'd never seen them all so grim and serious.

"April, are you sure you want to do this?" Jalil said quietly.

I laughed. "No. No, I'm pretty sure I do *not* want to do this."

Jalil's lips tightened into a frown. "Come back, okay?" he said.

"Okay, Jalil. If you say so."

"I do."

He squeezed my hand and went to stand with Mergon.

David rode in the lead, sword drawn. I was in the middle. Christopher brought up the rear, the horses for Baldur and Thor on leads behind him. The smell of death and decay was bad but the fear was worse. I tightened my hands on the reins.

"You know we are certifiably insane, you know that, right?" Christopher. "We are choosing, actually making the conscious decision to do this. That, my friends, is sick. Sick and wrong. I mean, we're talking the original charm school dropout here, guys. Miss Manners, the Junior League, Martha Stewart herself. Nothing's going to change this lady into something okay. She is one-hundred-percent, grade-A, extra-strength evil."

I blocked him out. He didn't need me to listen, anyway. Christopher was trying to calm himself.

David was quiet, tense, alert.

Me, under my breath I began to sing. It didn't matter what.

Then the song became another and then another. It was like all the words, the lyrics were tumbling together, all the melodies merging into one giant, mesmerizing chant. My head was filled with sound.

I'd cheated Hel once. Was I going to get to do it again. Or would I rot here forever?

Where was my faith when I needed it?

From behind me, Christopher spoke, his voice hushed but still high and giddy.

"Here's a question: Where is Merlin? Where is he? He was supposed to be here, why isn't he here?"

And then all hell broke loose.

CHAPTER
XXIV

They came from the ceiling, swooping toward us with tiny dark wings. One minute, nothing. The next, it was like the ceiling was peeling, these things scraping themselves off the surface and coming at us like a swarm of awkward, screeching bats.

"Holy crap!" Christopher shouted, struggling to keep three horses from bolting.

"What are those things?!" I cried.

Maybe guards or something? I thought. Hel wasn't stupid enough to leave any inch of her kingdom unprotected.

They were gargoyle-like creatures, about a foot tall, skinny legs and arms, webbed feet, clawlike hands, some with bellies extended, others whose ribs stuck out and stretched shiny gray skin. Their faces were hideously misshapen, decorated with mashed noses and sunken eyes and teeth as long and sharp as knitting needles.

And, of course, they flew on wings far too small to support them.

"Duck and keep going!" David shouted. "April, your sword!"

I bent close to the horse's neck, yanked Etain's sword from my belt and held it straight up into the air.

It wasn't enough. With a high-pitched screech the gargoyles reached us. One landed on my bent back, sank its needle teeth into my skin. I screamed, "Get it off, get it off!"

Our three horses were rump to rump now, crowded together, my legs bumping into David's on one side, Christopher's on another. The fourth and fifth horses pranced nervously on their lead. We were a tight mass of sweating horses and freaking humans.

I felt a horrible tear through my skin. The gargoyle was gone. David had ripped it off. I sat up, whacked at another one flying straight for my throat. Etain's sword cut through the gray flesh with ease. It fell with a thud to the ground.

Another came at me. I saw David swing his sword and the gargoyle's head dropped clean off.

Christopher twisted in his saddle. "David! I can't reach it."

A horrible animal scream! A gargoyle had landed heavily on the fourth horse and was sinking its teeth, vampirelike, into the horse's neck. The horse swung its head violently but couldn't dislodge the beast that was drawing blood through twenty tiny needles, causing twenty tiny dark rivers to flow. It tried to rear but couldn't, too close packed to the other horses.

Christopher started to dismount.

"Don't!" David ordered. "Let the horse go. Cut the lead and move on."

"Damn!" With a slash, Christopher cut loose the fourth horse. Still blindfolded, completely panicked, the horse backed away from us. It seemed to be what the gargoyles wanted. Because like a swarm of high-pitched buzzing bees, the remaining ten or so descended on the stranded animal, ignoring us.

What luck for us.

"Let's go, let's go!" David ordered. We did, not at a run, too dangerous with the horses unable to see and our not knowing what was coming next. But not at a stately pace, either.

"April, you okay?"

I nodded. My back burned with pain and I could feel the blood trickling, but I was alive. And we'd survived Hel's first test.

"Yeah."

Until the next obstacle Hel throws our way, I thought.

We rode on. The gargoyle-things didn't follow. I kept glancing at the rock ceiling, squinting in the almost dark, but saw none. Small lamps, not unlike those used in Baldwin's kingdom, were set in the walls at intervals of about ten feet now. If Hel meant to unnerve unwelcome visitors by making them wander through the almost unremitting dark, she was succeeding. At least as far as I was concerned.

"David?" I said. My voice echoed strangely off the walls. "Do we have any idea of where we're going? I mean, I'm assuming this path takes us to Hel. But what do we do if we come to a break in the road? Do we have any idea of which way to go? Do we have any idea of how big this place is?"

David's reply came low. "No."

"We're intrepid travelers, April," Christopher said. "We're just all carefree and jolly. When we come to a fork in the road, why, we'll just flip a coin or something."

I decided not to ask any more questions.

"Whoa!" David suddenly reined in his horse. It obeyed easily. It didn't seem to sense the suddenly new environment, didn't hear the howls or smell the feces and blood and death.

The scene before us was like something from an Hieronymous Bosch painting come to life — masses of men and women writhing in agony, limbs distorted, mouths open and howling, guts spilling and blood flowing.

"Great," Christopher said. "We go through that or we go back. Guess which I'm going to suggest we do. I'm not overly fond of the idea of becoming a hamburger."

David stared ahead, like he was trying to see something below or beyond the scene. "It's not real," he said, but he didn't sound so sure. "It's meant to frighten us back. But I don't think it'll hurt us."

"Are you sure?" I whispered.

"No. But no one's noticed us yet. Why? We're only a few feet away. It came out of nowhere. The horses aren't scared."

"Well, that works for me, General, doesn't it?" Christopher sneered. "The horses know best. Let's just wade right through this madhouse, this debauched slaughterhouse. No problem!"

I thought about it, though. "I think David's right, Christopher. I really want to go back and I can't believe I'm saying this, but we're kind of committed here."

"Yeah, yeah, I know. I'm just keeping my eyes straight ahead."

"Me, too," I said. I'd already seen certain acts of brutality I sincerely wished I had not seen.

"Follow me. Be ready," David said. He looked as sick as I felt.

The passage was psychological torture. Watching, trying not to watch, afraid we'd be pulled into the mess. But we passed through the scene unnoticed. No one reached out a bloody hand to yank me off my horse. No one — nothing — attacked. We were passing calmly through a living panorama of horror and abuse. A tableau of psychotic exploits. A ride from a lunatic's amusement park, complete with Smell-o-Vision and sound effects in Dolby Surround Sound. It succeeded in frightening me deeply.

When the last horse had stepped beyond the scene it disappeared. It was gone. Just vanished.

"Good call, David," Christopher said. Sincerely.

"Thanks," he said. "I think. But it's been far too easy so far. I don't like it. The worst is yet to come. Gotta be."

"David? Can you please hold back the happy act? Okay? Just this once?"

CHAPTER

XXV

We were now back in a dungeonlike place. Along the walls hung instruments of torture: belts and straps; manacles and chains.

"After that carnival back there, I am so not in the mood for an S&M joke," I warned Christopher.

"You know what, April? Me, neither," he admitted.

On a long wooden table lay a collection of what looked like butchering implements. Meaning, very large knives, some with long, skinny blades, like for cutting a fillet, others more like hatchets and machetes.

An Iron Maiden against one wall. A rack. And over another table, a very large, sharp blade on a pendulum.

"We obviously don't want to stay here," David muttered. "Let's go."

We did. Moved quickly through the chamber and into the next area. A wide, open space at the center of which was a massive pit of bubbling stuff, glowing like red-hot lava, emitting spurts of steam and shots of flame.

And suddenly, up out of the pit of fire and brimstone, stumbling out of the flames unburned — impossible — eleven men. Or what were once men.

"Freakin' *Night of the Living Dead,*" Christopher hissed. "*I Married a Zombie.* Get me out of here. I have seen enough."

The troop of figures stumbled toward us, beseeching, moaning. On each one the flesh was eaten away in places. Each one emitted the sickly-sweet stench of infection and decay. One man's stomach was a gaping and ragged hole, intestines spilling out and down his thighs. Another was missing both arms at the shoulders. A third man had been scalped almost down to the eyebrow ridge, the entire top half of his skull cut away. I'd heard the phrase "the walking wounded" used to describe people with a lot of emotional baggage. These men were *actual* walking wounded. There was no way, *no way* they could survive these wounds. Unless, of course, Hel was keeping them alive. Another one of her games of torture.

"What do they want?" I whimpered.

"They want us to put them out of their misery." David dismounted and held Galahad's sword at the ready, two hands around the hilt. Christopher and I dismounted, too. I don't know why.

"Can we?"

"We're going to try."

With a shout David charged the first man in the pack. He didn't falter or fall back. Just kept coming. There was a sickening sound as the sword slid through wet, oozing flesh. And as it came away, the new wound simply closed up.

Galahad's sword had no effect on these men.

David stumbled. The rotting man shoved him aside with a supernatural strength. David crashed to the ground and lay there, stunned. The men continued toward me and Christopher. Moaning, groaning, whimpering, their scabbed and sore-covered hands reaching for us. If Galahad's sword couldn't stop them on their desperate march, what could?

Etain's sword. Maybe.

But before I could find the nerve to reach for the sword, Christopher yanked me aside. "Watch out!"

The horses! David's and Christopher's and the

fifth horse, but not mine, were being pulled toward the pit! Their blindfolds had been ripped off and we could see their eyes wide and rolling, hear their frantic neighing, see their twelve hooves planted firmly but to no avail.

"No!" I shouted. I reached for the tail of David's horse, but it slipped through my hands.

And then Christopher grabbed me by the shoulders and forcibly turned me away so that I wouldn't see. But I heard. Horrible, horrible screaming and then nothing but the bubbling red stuff spitting and cracking.

I pulled away from Christopher.

Oh, God, the men were still coming! They were so close now, the stench unbearable. My stomach heaved, I gagged but stood my ground. I yanked the enchanted elfin sword from my belt. Pushed a suddenly frozen Christopher out of the way. The first man was only an arm's length away. It was now or never.

"April, no!" David yelled, coming to.

With a grunt that came from my feet I slashed at the first "man." His body fell a second later.

The other men surged forward.

And then it struck me: Was this a crime or an act of mercy?

Self-defense, April, another voice inside me cried out.

I lunged. Again and again. Eleven in all.

I shut down. April went away.

I watched as flesh suddenly melted away, like in time-lapse photography, and became muscle and tissue and ligament and tendon. Watched as that all melted away to become bone. Watched as the pile of skeletons was reduced to a smaller pile of dust.

I felt a hand on my shoulder.

"You had to do it." David.

Christopher. "Yeah. If it hadn't been for you, April . . ."

"Don't say it," I said. "Don't say anything."

We walked on. Christopher led my horse, the only one who'd survived. Still, Hel was nowhere to be seen.

"Biding her time," David said grimly. "She'll be here."

I tried to keep my mind focused on the ultimate task. Rescue Thor and Baldur. Get out of there.

David and Christopher remained silent. Before long, we found ourselves returned to the place we'd never thought we'd see again. Hel's "museum."

A collection of massive, craggy, blue-tinted blocks of ice. Like tall chunks of iceberg. Twelve on the left, twelve on the right. And in each block, visible through a smooth piece of slanted surface, a god. Sometimes a creature we couldn't identify.

This was Hel's cemetery for the undead, a graveyard for the barely living.

"Do we get them all out?" I asked.

"No time. We do what we came to do, no more. Later, well, we'll see who else we can save."

I started to protest. But David was right. I was being sentimental. We had no time.

"Hah. When hell freezes over," Christopher mused. "Not so impossible, after all."

"We get Thor out first," David said. "Then Baldur."

"Hang on," I said to Baldur as we walked past. Baldur was dressed like a wealthy Viking. He was tall, of course, built like a rock, and handsome. Hel herself had told us he was Odin's favorite, most beloved of the gods of Asgard. Baldur had said no to Hel's advances. She'd taken away his sword and locked him away in ice. Maybe she'd thought he was only playing hard to get.

We stopped before Thor's icy prison.

"Do you think he can hear us?" I said, looking into Thor's rigid face.

"Let's hope so," Christopher said. "I don't want to have to throw down with this guy. Something tells me I'd lose."

Oh, yeah. Thor was huge, god-sized, bigger by

far than Baldur. Bigger even than Loki in his most pumped and ferocious state. His arms were bare and had to be several feet around. His legs, encased in dark leather boots, could have been pilings for a house. His hair was long and wild and red-blond. Calvin Klein would have sold his soul to get that hair under contract.

Yes. Probably Christopher would lose.

David started to hack at the block of ice with Galahad's sword.

"Get ready to grab him when the ice breaks," David grunted. "He's got to be weak. His muscles broken down. And he doesn't have Mjolnir yet."

"Do gods have actual muscles?" Christopher asked, but he braced himself to catch the big god. "Well, it was nice knowing you, kids. This guy falls on me, I'm roadkill."

Ice splinters flew through the air. "Watch your eyes," David cautioned.

"Let's just get him on the horse," I said. "If the horse can hold him. Then we'll get the other one out."

And then, David's sword cut through the last quarter inch of ice. And with the eerie sound like a lake thawing, Thor half-fell, half-pushed his way through the opening.

"Look out!"

David and Christopher braced themselves

against the massive weight of the god as first one leg, then the other stepped through the shattered prison and onto the ground.

"Oh, sh —"

Christopher and David crashed to their knees, still trying to support Thor from each side.

"Can he stand?" I asked inanely.

"I . . ." The voice was a croak, but a god-sized one. "I can . . . stand. Thanks to these good fellows . . ."

Using David's and Christopher's shoulders as supports, Thor pushed himself to his full height. And swayed. David climbed to his feet and grabbed Thor's right arm. His fingers looked like twigs against a tree trunk. Christopher groaned, stood, and grabbed Thor's left arm.

"Uh, mighty Thor," I said, "we have to free Baldur and get out of here, fast. Can you walk? Try to take a step. We have one horse; we lost the others to Hel. . . ."

"Many thanks, good lady. But the mighty Thor will stand on his own feet. Who are you humans who have bravely entered Hel's domain in order to free me and my fellow god?" he said. His voice was already stronger but he didn't look too steady overall.

"We'll explain later," David said. "But we work

with Merlin. We're on your side. Now we have to get Baldur."

Still unsteady on his feet, but growing increasingly more used to movement after who knows how long, Thor followed us back to Baldur's icy prison. He insisted on helping smash the ice with his hands. He was more of a hindrance than a help. But even David didn't have the heart to ask him to stop. The guy was seriously grateful.

Finally, we heard the same desperate creak, and with a little help, Baldur broke free.

Whoever said real men don't cry is a fool. Okay, Thor and Baldur were gods, but they bawled in each other's arms with joy.

"I hate to break up this little love fest," Christopher said, "but we are going to be fried if we don't move. Now."

David nodded. "Right. Uh, we have to go, er, sirs."

Thor and Baldur pulled away from each other and wiped their eyes. "If only I had Mjolnir," Thor lamented, "I would stand and fight until Hel begged for mercy. And, of course, I would show her none."

"If only I had my sword," Baldur growled, "I . . ."

"If wishes were horses, fools would ride." The four of them looked at me. "What I mean is, come on!" I pulled on my horse's bridle. "Hel could be . . ."

And then, there she was.

Chapter

XXVII

I felt her first, a cold dark presence behind me. No mistaking who it was.

Automatically, the gods turned to face the threat.

"Thor, Baldur!" David yelled, refusing to turn with them. "Don't look at her face, keep your eyes down."

"Oh, crap, I knew this was not a good idea," Christopher said.

Hel.

A raging, rampaging goddess of death. One half of her body lovely and luscious and enviable. The skin firm and supple, the hair lustrous, the eye bright. The other half of her body, a rotted-out corpse, stuffed with maggots and worms, wet gray flesh hanging in flaps. A goddess capable of reducing men to quivering heaps of desire and loathing. Hel could drive a man crazy in an instant, tortured between all-consuming lust and overwhelming disgust.

No way could David and Christopher stand and fight and win. Especially when they also had to keep Thor and Baldur safe from Hel's grasp.

"Go, go, go!" I screamed. "Don't look at her, just go!"

They did. David and Christopher in the lead, with Baldur and Thor stumbling just behind, all four ran, panicked, back toward the Great Diggings.

Hel didn't seem to care. For some reason, I was the one she wanted. Just me.

But first, my horse.

"I saved this one for myself," she said gleefully. "I have been watching your progress through my kingdom, waiting for just this moment. And now . . ."

With an awful crash, my horse fell. I let go of the lead and jumped back.

The horse screamed once and was silent.

"How dare you interfere?" she asked calmly.

I screamed. Out of control, just screaming now, using words I rarely if ever had used, hurling insults like darts, yelling, yelling, yelling. My face was on fire, my limbs trembling, I just wanted to rip Hel apart with my bare hands, I was losing it.

Crazy to think I could do anything to really hurt her but I couldn't stop screaming.

Maybe she was a little stunned. Maybe the sight of a young human female so crazed with anger she was actually threatening a god caught Hel off-guard. Because she just stood there as I flung myself at her, Etain's sword held straight out in front of me, still screaming, now wordlessly, like my poor horse had screamed. Just one long awful shriek of rage and despair.

In the real world people in white coats would have grabbed me, wrapped me in a straitjacket. In Hel's domain, nobody could stop me. I charged straight ahead and saw only a glimpse of Hel's half-living face, absolutely stunned, before I plunged the sword into her living stomach.

It got her attention. Hel shrieked with fury. I yanked the sword from her stomach and stumbled back. Red blood flowed from the wound but suddenly, I was me again and I knew I hadn't really hurt her. Only succeeded in making her even more brutally angry.

"I know what you did to the eleven. You deprived me of a great pleasure, human," Hel spat.

I was down. Before I could blink I was flat on the ground, face up, staring at the monster above me. Hel stood with one leg on either side of me. On one side, beautiful, diaphanous robes. On the other, moldy, decayed fabric. A strip of gray flesh fell from somewhere under her robes, onto my chest.

Hel looked down at me and laughed. "All of your efforts, wasted. No *human* can conquer Hel. What, did you hope to rival me in beauty or in power? How foolish!"

Hel stepped away from me and pointed. Suddenly, I was bound by some sort of elastic material, trussed up like a roast ready to be stuck into the oven, hands and feet and arms and legs held motionless. With each breath I took, the ropes tightened.

I closed my eyes.

This was it, it was over. An eternity in hell, perpetual damnation and suffering beyond all imagining. Hel had me now in her horrible grip.

It was what I deserved.

CHAPTER
XXVIII

"Hold, daughter! Release the girl. It is I, Loki."

Dreaming. Hallucinating, that was it.

Carefully, I opened my eyes and tried to turn my head in the direction from which the voice had come.

It was Loki. And I was actually glad to see him. The Norse god of mischief and destruction. Loki had been the first god I'd met in Everworld. The first god to try to kill us. Now, he was my rescuer. My hero. Imagine that.

Loki stood about seven feet tall just then, large but not as large as he could get. The Ralph Lauren, model-perfect version of a Norseman, all blond and chisel-featured and hollow-cheeked, dressed in supple leather and gleaming chain mail. Loki was not a pleasant fellow. In fact, I'd decided a long time ago he was downright evil.

He was also ultimately responsible for the death of Sir Galahad, the perfect knight, someone I'd admired and maybe even loved.

Right then, however, I could have kissed him.

And then I saw that Loki was not alone. From the dark behind him stepped — Merlin. Not a prisoner. Things were definitely looking up.

"Listen to your father, woman," Merlin commanded.

"You!"

Loki rolled his eyes like a typical exasperated father dealing with a typical spoiled-rotten daughter. If I weren't so scared I'd have laughed. Hel was a handful. That's what my father used to say about Senna.

"The order of things has changed, daughter," Loki interrupted. He nodded at Merlin and his long blond hair fell over his shoulder. "I have come to see the wisdom of Merlin's way. All gods of every land must unite against the terrible forces of Ka Anor, that alien usurper. Together we will crush the alien cannibal and drive his followers, the Hetwan, from our lands. Together we will fight to preserve Everworld!"

"You will fight without me, then, Father," Hel replied simply. "The Queen of Terror rules alone and bows to no one." She sneered with the living side of her face. A maggot oozed from the lips on the dead side. "Especially not to a god who is weak enough to abandon his plan for domination in the old world in favor of the naive dreams of an old man!"

Loki swelled in response and it was incredible. He was huge. And it was probably safe to say he was pissed.

"A god has the right to change his mind!" he thundered. "In fact, daughter, I have the right to do anything I please, and you would do well to remember that. For example, if I choose to remove you from the throne of your underground kingdom, I will do so. Now, let her go."

"*Never!*" Hel gestured with her dead hand and a wet flap of putrified flesh slapped the ground inches from my face.

"Hel, you will listen to your father, Loki!" A new voice, a deep, rich voice. "And if you will not listen to him, you will listen to me, Odin, the All-Father. And if you refuse to listen to me, you will suffer greatly for your stupidity!"

I looked up again, a bit more brave.

Odin. I'd heard so much about him I was almost disappointed to finally see he looked pretty much like the other Norse gods, but older, more grizzled. Big, blond hair gone to grayish-white, handsome, a full beard. His clothes were far less elaborate than Loki's, and somewhat worn. After all, Odin had been imprisoned for a long, long time. But I also got the impression that Odin cared far less about fashion than Loki did, and far more about the important things. Like, at the moment, saving my life.

"No!" Hel shrieked. "This cannot be! Let me have this one girl, at least, mighty Odin. . . ."

"Hel does not bargain with the All-Father," Odin replied. His voice was absolute and dangerous. "Release the girl. And take yourself off somewhere out of my sight. We will leave this despicable place as we found it. Do you understand?"

Hel's reply was garbled by rage but she must have agreed to obey because suddenly, she was not there above me and the gutlike strings that bound my hands and feet and arms and legs were untying themselves and flying off.

Slowly, I sat up. In time to see Hel slither away with an entourage of goblins and other misshapen creatures.

Loki turned to Odin. "She is terribly spoiled and headstrong, that daughter of mine. I fear she will never find happiness."

I scrambled to my feet. Thought, *Happiness? Just how insane are you, Mr. Loki, sir? I don't think happiness is what Hel is all about.*

CHAPTER

XXIX

Leaving Hel's domain was an awful lot more pleasant than going in. Merlin, Loki, and Odin One-Eye, the All-Father, were my traveling companions now.

Merlin walked alongside me. Which was fine because I was pretty sure Loki and Odin had a lot to talk about, Odin having been Loki's prisoner for quite some time.

"What happened?" I said. "How did you get Loki to join you? How did you get him to release Odin?! Oh, and thanks for saving my life, by the way."

"It is a life worth saving," Merlin replied.

As we walked back up the dwarfs' tunnel to the safety of the Great Diggings, Merlin briefly explained how he'd located Mjolnir. That had been easy enough. Some Viking lord had appointed himself protector of Thor's special hammer until such time as Thor might return. Merlin had given the lord some gold coins in recompense and the lord had wept with happiness to learn Thor was about to be returned to his people.

Convincing Loki to release Odin and visit his out-of-control daughter had been slightly more difficult.

Loki had witnessed the murder of his son, Fenrir, by the Sennites. Had watched as his trolls turned tail and ran from the castle at Merlinshire. He'd learned that Senna was dead. His gateway was closed, for good. So if Loki couldn't leave Everworld, he might as well join forces with Merlin and Athena. Loki was not stupid. Merlin helped Loki realize that his best shot of survival lay with us.

Finally, the end of the tunnel was in sight. I could see the lights of Mergon's base.

I couldn't help myself. I started to run. I ran and ran until I stumbled out into the beautiful, gorgeous, never-been-lovelier dwarf homeland.

And met with a scowling, upset Baldwin.

"I'm back," I said unnecessarily.

"Yes, and what horrors have you brought with you?" he demanded.

I was confused. And then I got it. Baldwin had

seen Merlin and Loki and Odin go in. So far, I was the only one who had come out.

"Oh, don't worry," I gushed. "It's okay. Hel's gone. Everyone else is right behind me."

"Who is behind you?" Baldwin demanded.

David stepped forward and grinned. "Baldwin just got here. He doesn't know about Merlin and the others. He heard we'd prevented the tunnel from being sealed and came to give us crap."

I smiled. "Oh. Well, see for yourself, King Baldwin, sir."

I gestured behind me at the figures emerging from the tunnel. Merlin the Magnificent, followed closely by Loki and Odin.

Baldwin's face went pale. I could almost hear what was going on in his mind. *Oh, no. Now I am compelled to entertain not only the humans but a mighty wizard, as well. And not only two but four Norse gods! The cost to my coffers will be enormous! How will I ever afford a wedding feast. . . ."*

While Baldwin went to bow and scrape to his illustrious guests, I got the story from David.

David and Jalil and Christopher had held off the dwarfs and stopped them from sealing the tunnel. I hugged each of them.

"Good King Baldwin," Odin said, "you may release the barrier now. Hel has promised to behave but she is not to be trusted. Better to take all precautions."

Baldwin gave the order for the thousands of tons of rock and slag to be dropped and several of Mergon's crew entered the tunnel to obey his command.

And then Merlin presented Mjolnir to its rightful owner.

"I believe this belongs to you, mighty Thor."

The god took the hammer in his right hand and it was like watching a Christmas tree light up or a firework explode. The change was enormous and instantaneous. In a split second Thor went from a large, but weakened prisoner to a powerful warrior. He was charged with new life, infused with new energy. His body plumped, his skin began to glow, as if finally, after years of being packed in ice, the blood was once again warm and revitalizing.

Then Merlin presented Baldur with a sword. Baldur's transformation wasn't quite as immediate but it was dramatic, nonetheless. Gods always did things in a big way.

"I could use a little reanimating myself," Christopher said. "Not to mention a shower."

CHAPTER
XXX

I was so, so tired. So very tired but for the first time in a long, long time I was ending the day with a degree of hope. Finally, after so much despair, we had a fighting chance of driving Ka Anor from Everworld. Of uniting the gods with the help of Odin, Loki, Thor, and Baldur to free Everworld of the Sennites. I wasn't being naive. I knew we faced a long and arduous journey toward freedom, but hey, every journey begins with one step and we'd just taken a big one. Things weren't perfect, never would be, but that didn't seem to matter as much as it had when we'd first crossed over to Everworld. Maybe because now more than ever we were in charge of our future here.

I undressed. Then sat on the edge of the bed for a while, thinking. Letting my mind wander. For once the notion of what I might find there didn't terrify me.

I remember describing Everworld, back in the beginning, as a place not touching reality. How much had changed since then. Or maybe nothing had changed *but* me.

There's a famous saying, quoted by poets and other writers for centuries. "No man is an island." I'd amend that to "no person," but otherwise, I think it's true. None of us is truly alone. We live in relation to others, either in troubled times. Or peaceful ones.

But I think that at the major moments of transition, at the big comings and goings, something else is even more true. "You live and die alone." Just you, coming in and going out. Just you. Your choice to go back or move ahead.

I got under the covers. My head hit the pillow. And I slept.

February 18, 2001
Chicago, Illinois

Story by Jim Miller

Community Shocked by Disappearance of Five
Local Teens

A quiet suburban town is shocked and dismayed
by the mysterious disappearance of five local teens.
It is unclear at this time whether the disappearances
are related. The first disappearance occurred over
six months ago and the last, to date, on Saturday.

Though there is no evidence of foul play, friends
and family members continue to be questioned.

The teens, students at Crestwood High, are, according to Principal Robert Livington, all in good
academic standing and generally not considered
troublemakers. "If any of the five were having personal problems, the administration and faculty were
unaware of the situation," he said Monday morning.
"Their academic performances were steady and several of the five missing students were involved in ex-
tracurricular activities."

The first to disappear was Senna Wales of Rut-
land Drive. No evidence of foul play was found and
after a brief investigation, the police officially considered Wales a runaway.

The most recent to disappear was April O'Brien,
Wales's half sister. O'Brien is an A student, heavily
involved in the drama club, an active member of Our
Lady of the Roses parish, and a volunteer at several
nursing homes and shelters around town. Father
Michael Staub, a friend of and spokesperson for the
O'Brien family, says the family is devastated. "April
is not the type to run away. She is a happy girl with
a loving family and many friends. We ask anyone

with any information of April's whereabouts the day she disappeared to call the police. We pray for her safe return."

Second to disappear was David Levin of Newton Road, Wales's former boyfriend. His mother, a single parent, reported her son missing after he had not returned home for three days. Levin's father is retired from the U.S. Navy.

Christopher Hitchcock of Blackstone Street was reported missing by his parents when he failed to return home from school. A few days earlier, Hitchcock had been taken to the Lincoln Memorial emergency room suffering from a strange and as yet undetermined ailment. He was released into the custody of his parents. Hitchcock is also Wales's former boyfriend.

Jalil Sherman of Summer Drive, friend of Levin, was reported missing by his parents when they found a brief note in his room, addressed to his family. The contents of the note were released to the police. "It's not really helpful," admitted Detective William Costello, in charge of the investigation. "The note reads: 'It's okay. Please don't worry. I love you all.' Could be suicide, could be a runaway, could be anything." Sherman's father, John, suffered a heart attack late last week and is hospitalized at University Hospital.

Thus far the only connection police have among the disappearances is Senna Wales. "It might mean nothing," said Detective Costello. "But it might mean everything. We'll continue to investigate for as long as we can."

Anyone with any information about the disappearance of Wales, O'Brien, Levin, Hitchcock, and Sherman is asked to notify the police immediately. All calls will be kept confidential.

K.A. APPLEGATE

REMNANTS™

①

THE MAYFLOWER PROJECT

Up close, so near Earth, the Rock looked very small. Seventy-six miles in diameter, it was nothing next to the planet measured in thousands of miles.

But, up close, so close, Jobs could see the speed of it. Against the backdrop of space you couldn't sense the awesome speed. But now, as it angled into the atmosphere, in the brief second in which it could be seen outlined against blue ocean, it seemed impossibly fast.

The Rock entered the atmosphere and for a flash became a spectacular special effect: The atmosphere burned, a red gash in its wake.

It struck the western edge of Portugal. Portugal and Spain were hit by a bullet the size of Connecticut. The Iberian peninsula was a trench, a ditch.

The Mediterranean Sea, trillions of gallons of water, exploded into steam. Every living thing in the water, every living thing ashore, was parboiled in an instant.

Portugal, Spain, southern France, all of Italy, the Balkans, the coast of northern Africa, Greece, southern Turkey, all the way to Israel was obliterated in less than five seconds. They were the cradles of Western civilization one second, a hell of superheated steam and flying rock the next.

The destruction was too swift to believe. In the time Jobs could blink his eyes, Rome and Cairo, Athens and Barcelona, Istanbul and Jerusalem and Damascus were gone. Not reduced to rubble, not crushed, not devastated. This wasn't like war or any disaster humans understood. Rock became gravel, soil melted and fused, water was steam, living flesh was reduced to singed single cells. Nothing recognizable remained.

The impact explosion was a million nuclear bombs going off at once. The rock and soil and waters that had once defined a dozen nations formed a pillar of smoke and flying dirt and steam. The mushroom cloud punched up through the atmosphere, flinging dust and smoke particles clear into space.

Jobs could see a chunk of Earth, some fragment left half intact, maybe twenty miles across, spin slowly up in the maelstrom. There were houses. Buildings. A hint of tilled fields. Rising on the mushroom cloud, flying free, entering space itself.

The entire planet shuddered. It was possible to see it from space: The ground rippled, as if rock and soil were liquid. The shock wave was an earthquake that toppled trees, collapsed every human-built structure around the planet, caused entire mountain chains to crumble.

The oceans rippled in tidal waves a thousand feet high. The Atlantic Ocean rolled into New York and over it, rolled into Charleston and over it, rolled into Miami and washed across the entire state of Florida. The ocean waters lapped against the Appalachian Mountain chains, swamped everything in their way, smothered all who had not been killed by the blast or the shock wave.

People died having no idea why. People were thrown from their beds, dashed against walls that collapsed onto them. People who survived long enough to find themselves buried alive beneath green sea many miles deep.

Jobs saw the planet's rotation slow. The day would stand still for the few who might still be alive.

The impact worked its damage on the fissures and cracks in Earth's crust. Jobs watched the Atlantic Ocean split right down the middle, emptying millions of cubic miles of water as if it was of no more consequence than pulling the plug on a bathroom sink.

The planet was breaking up. Cracking apart. Impossibly deep fissures raced at supersonic speeds around the planet. They cut through the crust, through the mantle, deeper than a thousand Grand Canyons.

Now the Pacific, too, drained away. It emptied into the molten core of Earth Itself. The explosion dwarfed everything that had gone before. As Jobs watched, motionless, crying but not aware of it, Earth broke apart.

It was as if some invisible hand were ripping open an orange. A vast, irregular chunk of Earth separated slowly from the planet, spun sluggishly, slowly away. The sides of this moon-sized wedge scraped against the sides of the gash, gouged up countries, ground down mountains.

And now this wedge of Earth itself broke in half. Jobs saw what might have been California, his home, turn slowly toward the sun. *If anyone is left alive,* he thought, *if anyone is still alive, they'll see the sunrise this one last time.*

Earth lay still at last. Perhaps a quarter of the planet was bitten off, drifting away to form a second and a third Earth. The oceans were gone, boiled off into space. The sky was no longer blue but brown, as dirt and dust blotted out the sun. Here and there could still be seen patches of green. But it was impossible to believe, to hope, that any human being had survived.

All of humanity that still lived was aboard the shuttle that now slid slowly toward the distant sun. . . .

THERE IS A PEACE THAT SHOULDN'T EXIST.
BUT DOES.

EVER
WORLD

BY BEST-SELLING AUTHOR
K. A. APPLEGATE

- BDR 0-590-87743-7 #1 SEARCH FOR SENNA
- BDR 0-590-87751-8 #2 LAND OF LOSS
- BDR 0-590-87754-2 #3 ENTER THE ENCHANTED
- BDR 0-590-87760-7 #4 REALM OF THE READER
- BDR 0-590-87762-3 #5 DISCOVER THE DESTROYER
- BDR 0-590-87764-X #6 FEAR THE FANTASTIC
- BDR 0-590-87766-6 #7 GATEWAY TO THE GODS
- BDR 0-590-87854-9 #8 BRAVE THE BETRAYAL
- BDR 0-590-87855-7 #9 INSIDE THE ILLUSION
- BDR 0-590-87288-3 #10 UNDERSTAND THE UNKNOWN
- BDR 0-590-87000-X #11 MYSTIFY THE MAGICIAN

$4.99
EACH
(US)

Available wherever you buy books, or use this order form.

www.scholastic.com/everworld